Dead Channel

Dead Channel

Hanarden O. Bleu

Contents

Dedication

To the lost, the unheard,
and the damned who tuned in too late.
May the static never let you rest.

PROLOGUE

Before the voice, there was only silence. Not peace. Not stillness. Something deeper.

A silence that lived beneath the city, heavy as stone, older than memory.

The kind that listens back.

Thunder Bay sleeps.

Snow, soft and thick as wool, settles over rooftops and window panes. The lake lies still, black beneath the crust of ice, its breath hidden. The only sound is the low groan of an old transmission tower on the city's edge. Bent, rusting, wrapped in dead ivy, it leans like a forgotten sentinel.

At its base: concrete stairs. Chipped. Faint markings on the walls symbols scratched in old paint, long since drowned by mold. Below these stairs, a door. Locked for decades.

But the signal never died.

It just waited.

Beneath Thunder Bay is more than rock and ore. There is something buried, layered in fossilized voices, a frequency swallowed by time.

It once spoke through a thousand mouths. It was worshiped in the form of a song. And it was buried deep when man began to build with wire and steam.

But the right voice can unearth it.

The right tone, the right sorrow, the right mouth unaware of the god it feeds.

Tonight, the tower groans again. The silence stirs.

And somewhere, inside an old apartment cluttered with tapes and ghosts, a man dreams of static.

1

The First Broadcast

The box of tapes smelled like mildew and cigarettes.

Jack Morrow sat cross-legged on the warped floorboards of his apartment, snow drifting lazy spirals outside the windows. The old heater wheezed as if it were dying. He didn't care. His fingers, tremoring just slightly, traced the label on one cassette:

"Sleepwalk Canada – 2/17/14"

He remembered that night. God, he'd laughed so hard. A drunk woman had called in, swearing her cat could predict earthquakes. He played Portishead right after and made it sound like a prophecy.

That was the last year he felt like himself before Claire vanished. Before he checked himself into somewhere quiet, white, and drugged. Before his voice the only thing anyone ever loved went silent.

Now, it was just him. He and the tapes. He and the silence. And silence, he'd come to learn, wasn't absence.

It was listening.

He stood. The floor creaked like a warning. His boots were still wet from the walk earlier. He hadn't meant to stop at the old station. WCRX had been gutted. Stripped bare after bankruptcy. No one had used it in nearly a decade.

But when he passed it... Something called.

Jack picked up the portable recorder. Pressed PLAY.

The tape hissed. Then, his own voice:

"Midnight again, my sleepwalkers. This is Jack Morrow, and if you're hearing this... you're awake. Or something inside you wants to be."

He closed his eyes. God, he missed that.

Just then, the tape warped.

A new voice bled in over his own.

Not static. Not distortion. A whisper, raw and wet and wrong. It spoke one word.

"Jack."

He yanked the tape out. The machine kept spinning.

The lights flickered. The heater died.

And from the corner of the room, the radio dead for years lit up.

The needle jerked. Found 103.3 FM.

A woman's voice, soft and distant, filled the apartment like breath:

"I missed your voice, Jack."

His blood went still.

It was Claire.

But Claire had been gone for seven years. Swallowed in snow. Nobody. No footprints. Just a door left open.

Jack stood frozen, the sound of her voice filling the cracks in him like water in old stone.

"I'm still here," she whispered. "You just have to let me in."

The heater kicked back on. The radio went dark.

The tape had stopped spinning.

Outside, the wind howled like it knew something he didn't.

Jack Morrow sat down slowly, hands cold, eyes wide.

And for the first time in years, he whispered aloud:

"I want to go back on the air."

He remembered the way she used to sit on the floor with her back to him, towel draped over damp shoulders, asking him to brush her hair. The silence between them was then neither heavy nor haunted. It was soft. Domestic.

He would part the strands with fingers still smelling faintly of tape glue and microphone dust, and she'd hum along to whatever was playing always jazz, always out of tune.

"You'd make a decent hairdresser if you weren't already married to static," she'd once said.

He missed the weight. Not just her body, but her *presence*. The gravity she gave to a room.

Before Thunder Bay swallowed him whole, Jack Morrow was a voice.

Jack Morrow looked like a man half-faded, like someone time had tried to forget but couldn't quite erase. He was thin in the way grief makes a person thin gaunt cheeks, long fingers stained with ink and cigarette ash, eyes sunken but always searching. His hair curled around his ears in an unkempt mess, black with streaks of premature gray. The kind of gray that doesn't come from age, but from carrying the dead too long.

There was a time when Jack's voice could silence a room, when his poetry filled halls and hearts. Now it was hollow, cracked like a tape that had been played too many times. He wore the same coat every day: olive green, frayed at the cuffs, pockets full of old notes and broken pens. People used to say he looked like a romantic. Now, he just looked haunted.

He had been the late-night host of Sleepwalk Canada on WCRX 103.3 FM, a beloved station for the insomniacs, night owls, and the lonely souls who couldn't sleep with the world's noise. His voice was warm, inviting a quiet comfort in the dark. Jack Morrow had a way of speaking that calmed the restless. He knew how to listen. He had the patience of a saint, the charm of a man who made strangers feel like family. That was, until everything fell apart.

His wife, Claire, was a brilliant woman fiery, stubborn, and full of life in a way Jack could never quite match. She was the one who pulled him out of the spiral of cynicism he so often found himself in. They were partners in everything: Jack with his radio show, Claire with her studies in anthropology, always fascinated by the way the world moved, the way people lived and died. They were young when they met, fresh out of school, ambitious, and with nothing to hold them back.

But then, Claire disappeared without warning. One night, after a late shift at the station, she went out for a walk by the lake and never came back. The police search was brief. The ice-covered water, the wooded areas around Thunder Bay, all combed over. Nothing. Nobody. No trace. Just disappearance.

The days and months that followed were a blur for Jack. He couldn't remember how many times he'd turned on the mic and asked, in his best soothing radio voice, "Are you out there? Can you hear me?" hoping someone, anyone, would reply.

But the voice he spoke to most was his own.

His radio show lost its heart without Claire. It went from a warm, intimate show to something desperate, full of odd, off-beat rants. The station pulled him from the airwaves after too many complaints. The listeners stopped calling. The sponsors dropped out. And then, Jack... he vanished too.

Diagnosed with post-traumatic stress disorder, Jack was placed into psychiatric care for several years. He learned to quiet his mind with pills, therapy, and isolation. His connection to the world outside became thin, almost nonexistent. But he couldn't forget Claire. He couldn't stop wondering if she was out there somewhere, listening, waiting for him. He became obsessed with the why of her disappearance and the idea that something beyond the normal world was pulling the strings.

One afternoon, the doctors cleared Jack for release, saying he was "stable enough" to return to society. Jack agreed with them. He wasn't ready, but no one ever really is, are they?

Jack stood outside the crumbling, abandoned radio station, looking at the overgrown weeds poking through the cracked asphalt of the parking lot. He hadn't been back here in years, but somehow the station still felt like home. The boarded-up windows, the rusting antenna towering in the distance it all seemed... wrong. It was like the station had been waiting for him, silent but breathing beneath the cold earth.

Inside, the air was thick with dust and the sour smell of mold. Jack coughed as he stepped into the lobby, his boots echoing on the cracked tile floor. The walls were covered in peeling posters of old bands, faded flyers from long-forgotten events. There was no longer a receptionist. No one was here. The studio was deserted, like the rest of the world had moved on and left WCRX to rot.

Jack walked through the hallway toward the back of the building, where the old broadcast studio lay. It was barely recognizable, just a shell of what it had once been. The control board had long since been stripped, the microphones gone. But there, at the far end of the room, behind an old stack of discarded furniture, was a small, dusty hatch in the floor.

Jack crouched down, lifting the trapdoor to reveal a narrow stairway leading down to the basement. This was the place he had hidden his emergency backup equipment the generator, the radio transmitter, the equipment he had used to broadcast when they tried to shut him down. He could hear the hum of the old generator, still alive, still waiting.

He walked down the stairs, the cold concrete beneath his feet seeping through the soles of his shoes. The basement smelled like gasoline, oil, and old radio parts. Jack didn't even hesitate. He flipped the switch on the backup generator, feeling the familiar vibration as the room came to life. The red indicator lights on the radio gear blinked to life.

With a sigh, Jack sat in the chair, dusting off the microphone, his fingers trembling slightly. He didn't know why he was doing this. He hadn't thought about broadcasting again. Not in years. But here he was. He needed to hear something. Anything.

He spoke into the microphone.

"Good evening, Sleepwalkers. This is Jack Morrow, your late-night guide through the dark. If you're hearing this, you're awake. And you're not alone."

There was nothing at first just the hiss of static. But then... something strange began to ripple through the static. A faint whisper. A child's voice, far off but unmistakable.

"Jack... Jack, I'm still here..."

Jack froze, his heart hammering in his chest. The voice sounded familiar. Too familiar.

He waited. The whispers continued, faint but growing clearer. It was as if someone something was trying to break through.

"Jack... I'm still here... You didn't listen... You didn't "

The tape on the old reel crackled and tore. Then silence.

Jack didn't know whether to laugh or scream. His hands shook, his pulse racing. The voices sounded like Claire. But that was impossible. He had buried her memory so deep. So why why was she back?

Without thinking, Jack reached forward and turned up the volume, his eyes glued to the screen in front of him. He hadn't felt the presence of something so real in years.

But then, another voice this one harsh and strained, like it was fighting its way out of some unseen prison interrupted.

"Jack. You shouldn't have done that."

The air in the room seemed to grow colder. Jack's breath turned to mist in the freezing basement.

Suddenly, the lights flickered. Then blackout.

Thunder Bay in November was the kind of cold that got into your bones and didn't leave.

Detective Asha Varma stood beside the third burned-out car in as many weeks, its interior melted into slag, and the air around it still sharp with the sour tang of scorched rubber. She barely blinked as the coroner zipped the black bag closed and gave her a nod. They'd found what was left of the victim in the driver's seat mostly teeth, bits of bone, and a warped, old-school radio clutched in charcoal fingers.

She jotted the same words into her leather notebook that she'd written down at the last scene:

The victim was found burned. Radio nearby. No sign of struggle. No footprints. No sound.

Her breath fogged the air in short, controlled bursts. Asha didn't rattle easily. Detective Asha Varma was the kind of woman people underestimated until they heard her speak. Tall, broad-shouldered, with tired eyes and a jaw always set too tight, she moved through rooms like she didn't owe them anything. Her black curls were pulled into a low, functional bun, though a few always escaped, framing her face like soft defiance.

She still wore her wedding band. Still checked her phone for messages she knew wouldn't come.

Her grief wasn't loud. It lived in the way she clutched her coat tighter against the cold, in the silence after someone mentioned children, in the way she never turned the radio on in her car. Losing Emma had hollowed her, but not broken her. What remained was sharp. Purposeful. Dangerous.Ten years on the force, six of them in Missing Persons, and she'd seen what people could do when they broke. But this? This was different.

No forced entry. No suicide notes. Just gone.

Three people in three weeks, all within a few kilometers of each other. One was a college student, and the other was a nurse. One is a retired mailman. No known connection except for the static. Their phones recorded the same thing moments before they vanished or died: low-frequency static, garbled voices, and the faint sound of an old radio show jingle.

She had the tape on her phone. She hadn't told her captain. Not yet. But she listened to it every night in her car before driving home.

Something about it crawled under her skin.

"You're not alone. You're never alone... Sleepwalk Canada, 103.3 FM... shhhhhhhhhhhhhh "

Then came the sound of breath. Not hers. Not the victims'. Something else. Something behind the mic.

Asha's job was to find answers. Facts. Evidence. But the audio didn't follow the rules. It sounded like something reaching through the static. Something waiting.

That night, after hours, she sat in her tiny apartment concrete floors, half-unpacked boxes, and a single lamp casting pale light scrubbing the audio on her laptop with forensic software. Each time she slowed it down, new sounds emerged. Whispers beneath whispers. She layered and cleaned the file until a child's voice came through faintly:

"Don't listen. Don't let him back on."

Then another, lower, rasping, almost inhuman:

"Jack..."

The name chilled her. She didn't know Jack. Not yet.

But when she dug through Thunder Bay's records of long-defunct broadcasters, one name surfaced from a scanned newspaper clipping: Jack Morrow – "Voice of the Midnight" – WCRX 103.3 FM – Station closed following host's psychiatric hospitalization.

Asha stared at the screen, then back at the audio waves dancing on her laptop. The static pulsed like a heartbeat. Jack Morrow hadn't been on the air in nearly a decade. His station had been condemned, written off as a relic of a bygone era of late-night nostalgia.

So why were his broadcasts suddenly back?

The first time Jack heard Claire's voice on the air, she'd been dead for six years.

She laughs at his bad impersonations. She teases him about his radio "pillow voice." She kisses the mic once on-air.

Then gone.

Gone with no goodbye.

Now her voice returns. But it wears someone else's smile.

Jack offers sacrifices. Her comb. His blood. The mic is an altar. Static answers.

Each broadcast, his voice fades. Something else speaks.

One caller sobs for their mother. Another screams.

A voice recites the contents of Claire's suicide letter.

There was no letter.

He doesn't remember recording it.

The tapes are changing. Rewriting. Whispers grow clearer. The studio breathes.

Jack had once played a local ad so terrible that it looped the slogan three times by accident. "Thunder Bay Ford Built for Thunder. Thunder Bay Ford Built for Thunder. Thunder Bay Ford "

Claire nearly choked on her tea. "Play it again. Please."

They laughed for ten solid minutes, breathless and folded over the station desk like teenagers.

That laugh...

It was gone now. Stolen. And something else wore it like a costume.

He was alone. He was always alone now.

The air inside the condemned studio was thick with rot and mold, and yet the space around the mic felt sterile, as if time had forgotten this room. WCRX had been dead for a decade, just like his career, just like her.

But the signal came back.

It had crawled back.

Jack had powered the generator just to hear something again any-thing. He hadn't expected to find his voice waiting for him in the static. Not an echo. Not a recording.

His voice, saying things he had no memory of:

"Sleepwalk Canada... you're not alone... You never were."

The voice was slower than his own. Wet. As if it were being spoken through torn vocal cords.

Jack listened to that broadcast fifty times. And on the fifty-first, a sec-ond voice joined:

"Jack, I'm here."

Claire.

But not Claire.

It wasn't just the pitch. It was the cruelty behind the sweetness. The way she giggled between syllables, like someone was holding her mouth open and puppeteering the words.

That night, Jack resumed broadcasting.

He brought offerings: candles, old tapes, her hairbrush, and the bone comb she used. He cut his hand over the mic and whispered her name like a prayer. Static answered.

Then a child's laughter. Then a thump from the wall behind him.

The station was supposed to be empty.

He searched the building. Only rats. Or so he thought. But the next night, the back wall had a smear of blood on it, and pressed into the blood, five little fingerprints.

And the tapes began to change.

He hadn't recorded anything new, but reels labeled from 2007 now played content he didn't recognize. Voices begging. Crying. Screaming. Sometimes his own voice came through, whispering obscene things he'd never said. Other times, Claire's voice was layered in reverse, urging him to do something.

"You left me. Now bring them. One by one. Make them listen."

He tried to stop. Locked the studio. Burned the tapes. Slept in his car.

But every morning the door was open again. And the signal still live.

One night, after waking up in the booth with blood on his fingers and a blacked-out window of time, Jack checked the broadcast log.

It ran for six hours.

Uninterrupted.

The caller's audio was archived. That night's callers included:

- A sobbing child asking for her mother.

- A man screaming "GET OUT OF MY HEAD!" before a burst of static cut him off.

The whispers knew too much.

And now, things were moving in the static. Not voices. Not sound. Shapes.

Sometimes, Jack saw them just beyond the glass, shifting behind the reflection in the booth. One night, he blinked and a face pressed against the other side his own face, bloated and blue-lipped, staring at him through dead eyes.

He screamed.

He didn't remember running. He woke up on the floor of the control room, curled like a child, cradling the mic like it was her hand.

A new message had been carved into the wall.

"WE ARE BROADCAST."

The "we" was growing.

The more Jack spoke, the more the air felt crowded. The building seemed to breathe. His recordings grew wet, like someone was whispering into water. And beneath the whispers, something ancient began to groan a sound that felt geological, like a mountain sighing through the static.

He couldn't stop. He couldn't leave. Each night, the urge to return came like hunger.

And when he didn't show?

The signal played anyway.

2

The Third Disappearance

The boy's name was Noah Ellison.

Twelve years old. Quiet. Asthmatic. Bright, but chronically withdrawn. His mother described him as "a shadow with shoes." He'd disappeared two nights ago from his bedroom while his parents watched TV downstairs. No doors opened. No windows broken. But the only thing left behind was his crushed inhaler, as though it had been stepped on by something barefoot.

Asha stood in Noah's room at sunrise, letting her eyes sweep over the ordinary: baseball posters, dust-filmed shelves, and a flickering LED night light shaped like a fox. She didn't touch anything. She didn't have to.

The radio was still on.

WCRX 103.3 FM, long since removed from the registry.

All that was playing now was static, and the static was wet, as if it had passed through lungs to reach the speaker. Beneath it, she swore she heard breathing. Not Noah's. Not a child's. Something old. Slow. Patient.

"Did he listen to it often?" Asha asked, turning to Noah's mother, who stood in the hallway gripping a rosary.

"Every night," the woman whispered. "Even though it was just static. He said... he said the man on the radio was teaching him to speak backwards."

Asha froze. "What man?"

The mother's voice cracked. "He called him Father Frequency."

Down in the forensics lab, they enhanced a 3-minute recording from the old boom box. The tape hissed and popped. Silence for the first 30 seconds. Then:

"It's alright to be alone, Noah. All the brightest children are."

"Would you like to meet my family?"

"All you have to do is listen until the end."

Then came something else. A dragging sound. A wet snap.

And then Noah's voice.

But he was speaking in reverse.

The linguistics tech paled when he translated it:

"I see them on the ceiling. They're wearing my skin. I'm not done yet."

That night, Jack Morrow broadcast again.

He was thin now. Sallow. He hadn't eaten properly in days. His fingers shook as he adjusted the dial. The static greeted him like an old lover, rushing in with greedy arms. When he spoke, the mic didn't echo; it listened.

"You're back," Jack whispered. "You brought her again, didn't you?"

The signal giggled—a high, shrill warble like a child being strangled.

Then Claire's voice:

"Jack. Why didn't you check the basement?"

He froze.

He hadn't been in the building's basement since the night he reactivated the generator. That was months ago or weeks ago. Time was soup now. Jack left the booth with the mic still hot, descending the stairwell with a flashlight that sputtered more than it shone.

The door to the basement was already open.

Inside, the concrete walls wept moisture—a puddle spread from the back wall, thick and dark, smelling like rust and old breath. And there, nailed to the far wall, were dozens of cassette tapes.

Each one is labeled with a name.

Jack's hand hovered over a tape labeled: Noah.

He didn't remember recording it. But his handwriting was unmistakable. And something inside was scratching, not the tape ribbon—something inside the plastic casing.

He put it in his pocket.

That night, he played it live on air.

Back at her precinct, Asha listened to the same broadcast from her office, knuckles white, pen dropped, breath held.

First: static. Then a lullaby. Claire's voice singing in a pitch that peeled into ultrasound, vibrating the fillings in Asha's teeth. The lights in her office flickered.

Then Noah's voice, backwards again:

"The man has too many faces. He's wearing my father. He's eating the moon."

The transmission ended with a sharp burst of feedback like a scream played through a throatful of broken glass.

At the exact moment, emergency lines flooded with calls across Thunder Bay. Reports of missing pets, neighbors whispering in tongues, and black water leaking from kitchen sinks.

And a man was found wandering near Lake Superior with his eyes scooped out, humming "Silent Night" through his throat.

When asked his name, he only said:

"I am the tower. And the child belongs to the signal."

Back at WCRX, Jack finished the broadcast. He sat in the soundproof booth, hands trembling, mouth dry. But the signal didn't end.

Something else came through.

A face on the glass, Claire's, but half-rotted lips chewed open, her eyes just radio dials spinning in place. He screamed. But the booth was sealed. He fell to the floor, weeping, clutching the mic like a crucifix.

Then the static whispered:

"You've opened the gate, Jack."

"Now let them in."

Before WCRX became static and screams, it was just a signal, a lonely hum cut from the northern wind.

Thunder Bay wasn't the original site. It was one of several experimental locations chosen for a classified operation code-named Project Echo Seraph. On paper, it was atmospheric research funded through the Canadian Defense Research Board during the Cold War. In truth, it was a collaboration between military intelligence, fringe theologians, and a former Nazi radio engineer recruited during Operation Paperclip.

They weren't trying to send messages.

They were trying to listen for one.

In 1952, a broadcast license was quietly filed under the shell corporation Arclight Industries, which purchased a disused weather station outside of Thunder Bay. The structure was reinforced with underground access tunnels, triple shielding, and a Cold War-era generator rumored to run indefinitely without refueling. Engineers referred to it as "The Womb."

The directive:

Map the electromagnetic residue of human consciousness. Identify patterns—track anomalies. Replicate God's voice.

Radio became their altar. Signal became sacrament.

They called their system The Choir, a dozen subjects monitored and isolated, transmitting under sedation in soundproof rooms. The profiles varied: ex-soldiers with head trauma, autistic children with savant syndrome, and schizophrenics who spoke in dead languages. Many died within weeks.

Only one spoke back.

Patient #12, known internally as Conductor Alpha, was a teenage girl from Nunavut who had never spoken a word before entering the station. After forty-eight hours of continuous exposure to The Choir's frequency 13.33 Hz, she began speaking fluently.

But not in English.

Not in any language that anyone recognized at first.

When the tapes were reversed and slowed down, linguists identified phrases drawn from Latin, Babylonian, and a proto-Aramaic language, which was spoken only in temple ruins. She described seeing wires growing from angels' spines, and a man made entirely of echoes, whose face was a radio dial that was constantly spinning.

She gouged out her tongue on the edge of the mic.

She fed it to a crow that wasn't there.

She died smiling in the dark, clutching the antenna like a rosary.

Her final words, written in her blood, became legend within Arclight's black file archives:

"He rides the longwave and drinks the dial.

Father is coming. Turn the world upside down."

After that, the project splintered. A lead linguist disappeared during a live session, later found in the woods with his ribcage open like wings, his teeth embedded in the bark of a black spruce. Two engineers locked themselves inside the transmitter chamber and set it to maximum frequency. Their skulls ruptured from the inside.

Arclight was dissolved. Officially.

But the tower in Thunder Bay, the one WCRX operated from, was left intact, "awaiting decommissioning."

It never was.

No further reports were filed. No disassembly crews were dispatched. It simply... lingered.

And in 1971, late one night, a voice crackled back over the airwaves. A single phrase, repeated in a loop across the dead channel:

"Can you hear me now?"

No technician ever claimed responsibility.

Over the next decade, local folklore bloomed. Teenagers dared each other to sleep at the foot of the tower. Petitions were made to demolish it. Ham radio operators spoke of "ghost bursts" in the bandwidth around 103.3 FM, intermittent, impossibly fast voices that made listeners vomit, weep, or forget their names for hours at a time.

In 1983, WCRX was "resurrected" as a late-night indie station, fronted by a young radio host named Jack Morrow. He was told nothing of the tower's history.

But he dreamed of it.

He dreamed of the dial that bled, of static like laughter, of tunnels beneath the earth pulsing with heat.

Every night, he broadcast from that booth, the frequency bent closer to something not entirely human. Not entirely dead.

Now, ten years later, that old transmitter hums again. Reawakened by a man lost in grief. And somewhere in the guts of that station, beneath the concrete, beneath the bones, a presence stirs. Something that was never buried properly.

Something is still waiting to be conducted.

Later that night, Jack needed air. He wandered down to the street, coat flapping open, the breath in his throat raw like old paper.

That's when he heard it.

An ice cream truck. In November. No music at first, just the whine of the engine and the crunch of snow under wheels.

Then the speaker squealed and played a familiar tune.

Claire's lullaby.

"Hush now, little voice / Time to drift below..."

It looped, distorted, and slowed, dragging syllables like wet sheets across the air.

Jack stepped closer. There was no driver.

Inside the truck: nothing but darkness and two red radio dials where eyes should be, flickering like candles in a face he almost knew.

The speaker clicked.

"We all scream in the end."

Jack stumbled backward. The truck vanished into the fog.

He didn't speak for the rest of the night.

Jack had not noticed the hour slip away until he heard the faint click of the power switch. The hum from the old station transmitter filled the air once again, its static, unsettling in the way it vibrated in his chest, like a heart trying to break free from a ribcage.

He looked around the abandoned studio, everything coated in dust and cobwebs, his scent now mixing with the musty air, his lingering breath thick from alcohol. There was no immediate fear, no real rational thought—just compulsion.

For weeks, he'd been waking at strange hours with no memory of sleep, hearing the whispers before he even opened his eyes. At first, he'd thought it was just the isolation, the fog of madness consuming him.

But it wasn't. It was there, underneath, a presence that had only grown stronger since he'd turned the station back on.

Jack's hand hovered over the mic, trembling. The weight of what he was about to do pressed heavily on his chest, but the pull to speak, to call, was irresistible.

He leaned in, and his voice cut through the static, barely audible.

"WCRX, Thunder Bay. Is anyone out there?"

There was no immediate response. Only the soft buzzing of electricity, the hum of wires older than he was, the flicker of dead light fixtures above. He exhaled sharply, trying to quell the panic rising in his throat.

Then

A voice.

Faint at first, lost in the undercurrent of static, like a child calling out for help.

"Jack... Jack Morrow... Do you... Remember?"

The hairs on the back of Jack's neck stood straight. His hands were slick with sweat, fingers freezing against the microphone. The voice... It wasn't just the crackle of a bad signal. It was something more.

"Claire?" His voice cracked, a mixture of desperation and disbelief.

No answer. Only the chilling buzz filled his eardrums. The voice that had once been Claire's, now hollowed and distorted, like it had come from the depths of a grave.

The lights flickered overhead as if the power itself was trying to reject the transmission.

"WCRX, Thunder Bay," Jack repeated into the mic, struggling to keep steady. "I don't understand. What do you want from me?"

The response was louder this time. It filled the room with a guttural growl, low and far too human to be a mechanical error.

"You're not... supposed to be... here."

Then, silence.

But Jack didn't move. He didn't pull away from the mic. Something told him he needed to wait, needed to hear more.

And then it came. Not in words, but in sounds: scraping, shuffling, like something significant was stirring beneath the ground. A slow, grinding rhythm, like a creature inching closer, inching through the very frequencies that clung to the walls.

It was quiet the next morning.

Too quiet.

Jack sat in the booth, staring at the mic, untouched coffee cooling beside him. No voices, no whispers, no warping of time. Just the soft hum of the generator and the ambient creaks of an old building remembering how to settle.

He should've felt relief.

Instead, he felt watched.

He adjusted the mic, not to speak, but to listen. Held his breath. Closed his eyes.

Nothing.

He leaned back. The silence wrapped around him like a wet sheet.

For the first time in days, Jack reached for a record.

Billie Holiday.

He placed the needle down gently.

◈ *I'll be seeing you... In all the old familiar places..* ◈

The crackle of vinyl joined the silence, and for a brief moment, Jack remembered normalcy.

Claire had loved this song.

He almost smiled.

Then the lights flickered just once.

And from the hallway outside the studio, a whisper:

"You used to play this when she cried."

He stood, spine locked.

The hallway was empty.

But the record kept playing, steady and unbothered.

3

The Arclight Files

S ubject: Conductor Alpha (Patient #12)
    Date: February 5, 1963
Location: WCRX Radio Tower, Thunder Bay
File Redacted
Security Clearance: Level-4
Operation: Project Echo Seraph Phase III Transmission Initiation

---

Subject: Conductor Alpha

Patient #12 was administered an experimental regimen of audio frequency exposure via Project Echo Seraph. The intent was to induce altered states of consciousness through continuous high-intensity radio waves. The subject was pre-screened and selected for their unremarkable mental health history, showing no signs of psychosis or cognitive deviation. Initially, the patient underwent several stages of observation, all of which were marked by standard behavior.

Timeline:

Day 1: The Subject underwent initial exposure to static frequencies at 5kHz. The subjects' sleep cycle began to break down—no signs of distress were evident. Minor speech disturbance reported.

Day 2: Exposure increased to 13.33 Hz. The subject begins to exhibit erratic speech patterns. Claims to be hearing "voices from behind the static."

Day 3: Subject begins to speak in a mixture of reversed Latin, Old Church Slavonic, and an unknown dialect. Attempts to communicate the name "Father" and references to "long waves" and "dials." The subject physically distorts during speech, with their facial features appearing to melt and reform.

Day 4: Subject gouges out tongue using fingernails and consumes it, claiming it was "offered to the crow." The on-duty technician in the room sensed an unknown presence—no physical evidence of the crow.

Final Log: Subject appears to understand her state of death. Final words: "He rides the longwave and drinks the dial. Father is coming. Turn the world upside down."

Redacted Addendum:

Subject #12 was not the first to show signs of connection. Previous subjects who reached similar states reported similar claims: a figure calling itself "Father." Victims who were exposed to the frequency for over 48 hours were found missing, often leaving only their teeth behind.

Project Echo Seraph was decommissioned, but not before several additional subjects went unaccounted for. Arclight Industries made the final decision to terminate the operation.

However, the transmitter in Thunder Bay remained operational.

And as of last year, unauthorized signals were detected again.

Redacted File Received by Detective Asha Varma

(Document Summary)

Subject: Investigation into Disappearances
Case: 2347-420-AC
Investigator: Detective Asha Varma

Case Summary:

A series of disappearances have been tied to a strange common thread: all victims were last seen listening to old radio frequencies, predominantly 103.3 FM, once operated by WCRX.

Initial findings suggest a link between the location of the station and the frequency of 13.33 Hz. Early autopsies on the bodies of victims display similar post-mortem abnormalities: ruptured ear canals, expanded skull fractures, and a high level of unexplained radiation exposure. All victims are missing tongue tissue, although no signs of trauma exist.

Personal Note:

I have reviewed several testimonies from local witnesses who reported hearing strange whispers and distorted voices through old radios, even after the station had been shut down. One elderly woman spoke of her son, who had been obsessed with the frequency for weeks before his disappearance. He talked about hearing a voice that "called him home." I believe there's more to the story. WCRX was closed due to its association with classified government operations. There is a definite connection between this frequency and the deaths.

I am continuing to dig into the station's past, and I suspect that whoever or whatever is responsible for these deaths is still linked to the tower. I believe there is a demonic entity using the frequency to reach into the minds of those who dare to listen.

Detective Varma's thoughts were interrupted as she stepped into the quiet office, the hairs on the back of her neck standing up. She could feel it, the presence, the same she'd felt when she first heard the reports of the disappearances. She didn't know how, but the signal was coming for her now. too.

The small, sterile office felt as if it had swallowed Asha whole. It wasn't just the coldness of the room; it was the weight of the mystery that pressed against her chest, suffocating her with every breath. The file she held felt heavier than any piece of evidence she'd ever worked with. It wasn't just a case. It was a warning.

Flipping through the pages again, Asha couldn't shake the feeling that this wasn't simply an investigation into a series of disappearances. This was something much darker. She ran her fingers over the edges of the pages, the smoothness of the paper only heightening the eerie silence in the room. The file was full of redactions, but one thing stood out amidst the gaps.

The word "Father."

It was everywhere. The victims had whispered it. The reports mentioned it. And now, as she read the police report about the body found behind the house, she could feel it in her bones. It wasn't just an accident or a brutal murder. This was something otherworldly.

Asha looked at the time on her phone, the dim glow casting eerie shadows across her desk. She had been here for hours, but the longer she stayed, the more the walls seemed to close in on her. The stale air in the room thickened, almost tangible, as if it were alive. A cold breeze brushed her neck.

The dead body described in the report had been found mutilated. No tongue. No identification. But it wasn't just the absence of identity that haunted Asha; it was the presence of something she couldn't quite explain—the feeling. The file described a body "twisted unnaturally" and "grotesque beyond recognition," but she knew there was something the police hadn't written down. Something they didn't understand. This wasn't just the work of a sick mind. It felt like an entity had been involved.

She ran a hand through her hair, trying to clear her head. That's when she caught the name again. Father. The same name that had appeared in the final words of the murdered victim, scribbled in blood. The same name that Jack Morrow had muttered, though it had seemed more like a desperate plea than anything else.

Jack had been connected to all of this somehow, whether he realized it or not.

With a sudden surge of determination, Asha stood up, pushing her chair back. She needed to see him. She needed to understand what was happening. Her instincts screamed at her to act quickly, before whatever this thing was had a chance to spread further.

Asha grabbed her coat and hurried out of the station, not bothering to lock the door behind her. The air outside hit her like a slap to the face, but it was a welcome shock, a brief reminder that the world hadn't completely tipped over into madness. Not yet. But it would be soon if she didn't figure this out.

Her car's engine sputtered to life as she backed out of the parking lot, the sound of the tires screeching against the pavement sending a sharp jolt of anxiety through her.

Something was waiting in the dark for her.

Jack sat in front of the glowing radio equipment, staring at the flashing dials. The station had been dead for years. He had made sure of that. The dark, decrepit walls of WCRX 103.3 FM loomed around him, the air inside thick with the scent of mildew and old metal. It felt like the building itself had been rotting for decades, but Jack wasn't bothered. He was beyond caring about things like decay and the passage of time.

The hum of static filled the room, buzzing in his ears like a thousand gnats flying in a circle around his skull. The emptiness around him was absolute, like the quiet of a tomb.

But the quiet had changed.

It wasn't just static anymore. The air was thick with a different kind of presence. It pressed against his chest like the weight of a thousand eyes. Jack's hands trembled as they hovered over the microphone, the cool metal of the mic stand now feeling uncomfortably alive under his fingers.

It had started slowly, the whispers. Just faint sounds under the static. At first, Jack had dismissed it. Probably just interference. But no, the whispers had grown clearer, becoming more distinct. He thought he could hear his name.

But then came the voice.

It was faint at first—a child's voice, soft and plaintive, calling for help. The voice had felt familiar, too familiar, and Jack had almost convinced himself it was just a trick of the mind until it started speaking his old catchphrases—the ones he'd used to close his late-night shows.

"Stay tuned... It's not over yet," the voice said, echoing his own words.

Jack's breath caught in his throat.

He reached for the dials, twisting them furiously to try and clear the signal, but it only grew worse, more insistent. The voice turned into something darker. It started saying things he'd never said. Things he couldn't remember.

"Come closer, Jack."

It was a growl now, distorted, like a demon dragging itself through a pit of broken glass. His stomach turned. He could almost feel the weight of it, that unseen presence pushing into the room, suffocating him with its intensity.

Jack tried to speak into the mic. He had to stop it. He had to shut it down.

But the words wouldn't come. His throat was dry, too dry. A crushing pressure filled his chest, and it felt as if the very air had become poisoned with something foul.

Then came the word he feared most.

"Father."

The voice called it, calling it like a name, Father. It was the same word he'd heard in his dreams, the same word his wife Claire had spoken before she vanished. He couldn't escape it. The feeling, the sensation of being watched, had become unbearable. The air was thick with it.

Jack's hands were shaking now. Sweat beaded down his neck. He reached for the dial again, desperate to shut off the signal, to cut the connection. But before he could, the room shook. The walls cracked. It felt like the building was alive, its very foundation groaning beneath the weight of something unseen.

The radio hissed louder.

Father.

A cold wind swept through the room, howling through the cracks in the walls. Jack's fingers were cold and stiff. He reached out for the power switch, but it was no use. Something was there, pulling him closer, dragging him toward the mic. It wasn't just the static anymore. It was a presence, a being, something ancient that had been waiting.

He couldn't escape it.

And then, in a voice deeper than any sound he had ever heard, the thing spoke:

"Father is coming. Turn the world upside down."

Jack collapsed in the chair, his head spinning, his mind unraveling. The mic was alive now. It was pulsing with energy, the frequency vibrating through his skull like a thousand needles. And the words kept repeating, over and over again.

Father. Father. Father.

Something was coming. And it wasn't going to stop until it had him.

That same night, across the city, Asha sat in her car outside her apartment, engine idling. She hadn't turned off the ignition yet, fingers clenched around the steering wheel, teeth grinding with exhaustion.

She closed her eyes. Just a minute, she thought—just one.

The radio came on.

She hadn't touched it.

No station. Just static.

Then:

Her voice.

"I don't believe in ghosts. I believe in patterns."

Asha's eyes flew open.

She'd said that earlier. In the precinct. To no one but herself.

The static warped and crackled.

"Stop digging. You're next." Her voice again. Same tone. Same breath.

She reached to shut the radio off.

It growled.

"I know what you saw on the tape. I know what you dream about. He hears you thinking."

The ignition cut off on its own. Lights flickered. Her rearview mirror cracked.

Then silence.

She got out, breathing hard, forgetting to lock the door.

Inside her apartment, the light on her answering machine blinked red—one new message.

When she pressed play, it whispered:

"Good evening, Detective. This is WCRX... and we're inside your walls.

4

The Broadcast Spreads

The hour was always the same.

03:00 a.m. sharp. The witching mark. The breath between yesterday and now.

In Jack Morrow's basement, where mold climbed the concrete like veins under skin, the only light came from the soft orange glow of the radio's ancient dial, humming softly like a heart murmur. The equipment was obsolete by any sane standard, yet it crackled with life, sullen and steady, as if fed by something older than power.

Jack sat hunched over the mic like a penitent priest at the altar. The turntable before him spun with aching precision, the stylus sliding into the first grooves of a record older than his memory. The room smelled of dust, vinegar, and electricity. And under it all, static. That ever-present layer of sound, blanketing the silence like snow on a fresh grave.

He pressed the "On Air" switch with a reverence that bordered on devotion.

The red light blinked.

The signal flowed.

Something deep in the frequency range yawned open.

"Good evening, friends," Jack began, voice low, intimate, caressing the edge of a whisper. "This is WCRX, broadcasting from somewhere between the pines and the pain. I'm Jack Morrow, and tonight... we remember what it means to listen."

He paused.

The silence stretched uncomfortably, unrelenting like a stare held too long. The soundproof walls seemed to lean inward.

The record spun, slow and warped. A crooner's voice poured through: I'll be seeing you... In all the old familiar places...

Jack's fingers traced the knobs absently. He hadn't scripted a show in weeks. He barely remembered showering.

Each night, he returned to this ritual like a fever dream. Each night, the voices returned louder.

Not the callers. Not the listeners. Something else.

He lit a cigarette, the ember casting a faint halo over his hollowed face. Shadows clung to his eye sockets. His beard had grown wild and uneven. His skin had taken on a gray pallor, like a body half-dragged from the lake.

He turned the mic back on.

"I had a dream last night," he said, eyes locked on the soundboard as if afraid to blink. "I was underwater. I could see the stars above, flickering through the ripples. I tried to swim upward, but my arms felt like they were made of wires. I heard her voice."

His breath hitched. His voice cracked around the next word:

"Claire."

The name echoed in the still room, followed by a ripple of static that wasn't his doing.

He froze.

Then, like a whisper choked through metal, her voice bled through.

"Jack... you left me in the dark..."

He turned pale. The mic wasn't open. His headphones lay untouched. And yet... it was there. Not an echo. Not a memory. Claire's voice.

"I waited at the water's edge. You never came back."

Jack staggered backwards.

She'd heard something that first night. A voice that made her childhood nightmares feel like lullabies.

Her eyes flicked to the photo pinned above her desk, Claire Morrow, declared dead five years ago. Nobody. No trace. And now, her name was surfacing again... in whispered testimonies, journal entries, voicemail glitches.

Asha stood up, grabbed her coat, and left without locking the door.

She needed answers.

She needed to find Jack Morrow.

And whatever was crawling through the wires behind his voice.

His chair was knocking over a stack of vinyls. They scattered like black mirrors, reflecting nothing at all. He clutched the table, white-knuckled, panting. Sweat rolled down his temple.

"No," he muttered. "You're dead. You're gone."

The radio began to swell with static so deep it sounded wet. Gurgling. Swallowing.

Then came a second voice, not Claire's. No human voice. Something vast, a chorus of insectile tongues whispering in unison from beneath the floorboards of the world.

"She is only the beginning. Keep speaking, Jack. Keep calling. You are the keyhole. We are the mouth."

Jack screamed.

And in that scream, the static answered.

The basement lights flickered, dimmed, and went dark. But the radio stayed on.

The signal was alive.

Meanwhile...

In a cramped, overheated office above Thunder Bay's fading city hall, Detective Asha Varma stared at another missing person file. Third one this week. Mouth sewn shut. Eyes crusted with gray ash. Fingers burned into a "shhh" gesture.

They'd all last been seen late at night. Radio is still playing beside their remains.

WCRX.

She circled the call letters again, teeth grinding.

It was impossible. That station was dead.

And yet... her radio, off and unplugged, had started tuning into it at midnight.

The call came at 3:33 a.m.

Detective Asha Varma was already awake, sitting on her couch with a cold cup of green tea untouched beside her. She had fallen into a pattern awake long after midnight, as if her body was reacting to something unseen, something waiting just past the hour.

The dispatcher's voice was thin, metallic. Another one. Found by a jogger, riverside. And it was bad.

Asha arrived before forensics did. The corpse sat propped beneath a black pine tree, legs folded unnaturally, mouth slack and frozen mid-scream. His fingers were bloody stubs chewed down to bone. The flesh around his lips was torn in vertical streaks, as if he had tried to rip his mouth open wider. Or someone had tried to reach in.

A small, battery-powered radio buzzed beside the body.

It was still on.

The signal wasn't a proper station, not by any tower in Ontario's network. Just static. But not flat white noise, something layered. There were rhythms. Shapes. Hidden beneath it, a voice pulsed in low, wet syllables.

Asha turned away as the smell hit her—burnt copper and ozone.

Then she noticed it. The man's skull was scorched, like someone had branded the bone itself through the skin. The scalp had cracked and peeled where the fire met it, curling like dry parchment.

Etched into the frontal plate, barely visible beneath the gore, was a word:

FATHER

She knelt close, flashlight sweeping over the symbols. The heat pattern was too precise to be accidental. It wasn't fire. It was sound—an acoustic burn.

She'd seen something like this once, in an old CSIS archive, a redacted document from the Cold War. Unexplained cranial etchings in psychic warfare experiments. They had called it resonant scarring. She hadn't believed it then.

Now it stared up at her, etched in bone.

Back at the precinct, she ran prints. The man was Evan Krall, 29 years old. Night shift manager at a nearby mill. No criminal record. No mental health history.

She scanned his social feed. Three nights ago, he posted a single story, grainy and low-res. A radio tuned to static. The caption read:

"Some guy's back on the air again. Same voice from when I was a kid. Jack Morrow?? Holy sh*t, didn't he die?"

The post was timestamped: 11:59 PM.

Asha drove to the archives building just after sunrise. The walls smelled of dust and formaldehyde. She had a file she'd requested weeks ago, something she hadn't expected to need: Arclight Industries: WCRX Records, 1952–1971.

Most pages were heavily redacted, names blacked out. But a few remained intact.

"The voice does not merely transmit through signals. It reshapes the brain's ability to hear. Then, it implants."

"Subjects begin reporting hallucinations as dreams first. Then voices. Then ideation of harm, not self-directed. Harm toward others... and the body's boundaries."

"Final state is uniform: voice-induced cortical burns. Subject 12's final words matched Subject 4, despite years apart."

He rides the long wave and tunes the dial. Father is coming. Turn the world upside down.

That night, Asha tuned in.

She found it. Just past 103.3 on the dial, a whispering not meant for the human ear.

Then Jack's voice came through. Gentle. Familiar. Ruined.

"Good evening, Thunder Bay. You're not alone anymore. Let's go deeper tonight, shall we?"

"Let's open the door."

The midnight hour had long passed, but Jack hadn't noticed, and time had become a foreign concept, slipping away like sand through a clenched fist. The dim lights of his basement studio flickered, casting eerie shadows on the walls, as his fingers rested on the microphone. It was no longer a choice. It was instinct.

Tonight, as every night now, Jack spoke as if he were feeding his madness through the airwaves, his words draped in the thick veil of static. His voice trembled with a tremor of longing that no one could hear except for himself.

"Good evening, lost souls. Can you hear me? Can you feel me in the dark? We're all alone, aren't we? All of us... alone in this hollow world."

He paused, listening to the silence that followed, to the hum that grew louder, deeper, a pulse that seemed to vibrate from the very air itself. But then, amidst the static, her voice came—Claire's voice.

"Jack... you're here... I'm still here."

His heart skipped in his chest, his breath catching in his throat. He had heard her before, faint whispers at first, echoes buried beneath static. But tonight, it was different.

The voice was more substantial, more transparent, more tangible than before. It was as if she were standing in the room with him, her breath warm against his skin.

"Claire," he whispered, his voice cracked, his eyes wide. "I... I don't understand. You... you're dead."

The room seemed to close in on him, the walls breathing, the air thick with something unholy. His hands, trembling, gripped the mic with a desperate force.

"Jack," she whispered again, but this time her voice was warped, a low, guttural rasp beneath the softness. "You have to listen... I'm so close..."

His vision blurred, the shadows around him twisting into shapes that moved just out of sight. The signal hummed louder, vibrating in his bones, seeping into the marrow of his soul. It was pulling at him, calling to him, deeper than he had ever been before.

He staggered to his feet, hands reaching out, feeling his way through the dark. "Claire... I don't know what you want from me."

And then it came. A flood of whispers, hundreds of voices overlapping old, young, male, female, all of them twisted, broken. Their words were incomprehensible, but Jack understood the feeling they carried. It was hunger. A need. A thirst that would not be quenched.

"Please," he begged, dropping to his knees, his body shaking with an uncontrollable tremor. "I need to know. What are you? What have I... what have I unleashed?"

The static pulsed again, louder, like a heartbeat, and Claire's voice returned, no longer sweet, but demanding, commanding, her tone now cold and suffocating.

"We are all waiting for you, Jack. Come. Come to us."

The words hit him like a physical blow. He gasped for air, his chest tightening as he collapsed back into his chair, his eyes wide with terror. The mic crackled with life, but now it wasn't his voice that echoed through the speakers. It was something darker, more profound, something that resonated in the very fabric of the world itself.

He heard it then. A sound so horrifying, so unnatural, that it made his skin crawl. It was a growl. No, a growl would have been too easy. It was a gnawing sound, a vibration that scraped at the edges of his mind, pulling his consciousness away from his body. It was the sound of something ancient, something that had been buried for centuries, a creature that had existed before humanity had learned to speak.

And in that moment, Jack realized what he had done.

The Mouth Beneath had woken. And it was hungry.

Meanwhile, Asha sat in her office, the fluorescent lights buzzing above her head, casting an unnatural glow on the manila folders strewn across her desk. The case of the disappearances had led her down a rabbit hole of confusion, and she was beginning to realize there were things far worse at play than simple crimes of violence.

The latest file on her desk was a redacted report from an old, classified investigation into Arclight Industries. The file was thick with black bars, but some information was still legible. As she flipped through the pages, her eyes caught a name she recognized from her recent inquiries into WCRX.

Jack Morrow.

Her fingers hesitated over the page, and she leaned in closer, reading the following lines:

"...Subject: Jack Morrow, previously employed as a late-night radio host. The patient exhibits signs of dissociation, severe grief-related trauma, and auditory hallucinations. Symptoms suggest the subject may have been exposed to an electromagnetic anomaly of unknown origin... or perhaps it's a much older force."

The words were chilling. Her fingers trembled as she flipped through more pages, each one detailing the strange and inexplicable behaviors of the station's employees, of the psychics and mediums involved in the original broadcasts. And then she found an audio log from one of Arclight's earliest tests. It was marked WARNING: HIGHLY CLASSIFIED.

She pressed play on the ancient cassette recorder, the sound crackling through the speakers, warped by years of neglect. At first, all she heard was static, but then... then she heard something else. Something primal. A whisper that crawled into her bones.

"Father is coming. The Mouth awaits."

The voice was faint, distant, but Asha felt the hairs on the back of her neck stand up. She rewound the tape, her mind racing. The Mouth. The Mouth Beneath. It was the same voice she had heard in Jack's broadcasts.

Suddenly, the weight of the truth settled in her stomach, heavy and cold. The signal, the disappearances, the mutilations, all of it was connected. Jack wasn't just a man lost in grief; he was the conduit, the last key to unlocking something far older, far more dangerous.

And she had to stop him before it was too late.

The night air outside was cold, too cold for late summer. Jack's breath clouded as he stepped out of his basement studio, his feet dragging through the shadows that clung to the house like a festering wound. He hadn't slept in days, maybe weeks. Time felt irrelevant now. Each night, he returned to the mic, to the hum, to the whispers that grew louder, more demanding, more insistent.

Tonight, though, something was different. There was a chill in the air that wasn't just the temperature; it was the kind of cold that gnawed at the bones, made the hairs on the back of your neck prickle with an unmistakable sense of wrongness. As he stood in the doorway, staring out into the empty street, he could feel it.

Someone was listening.

Someone was out there.

And they were never going to leave.

Back inside, Jack slumped into the worn chair in front of his old, static-filled console. The low buzz of the radio greeted him like an old friend, its crackling voice beckoning him into the dark. His fingers trembled slightly as they hovered over the dials, adjusting the frequency. He had started to notice something, a strange dissonance that didn't fit like a frequency that shouldn't be there, something he hadn't dialed, something that shouldn't exist. It was more than just static. It was a presence. And it was growing.

His mind raced, his thoughts scattered like broken glass. The signal was different, older, far older. It wasn't just the frequencies he knew, the ones tied to wires and towers. No. This was something that crept beneath the surface of the world. Something that didn't need technology to spread.

Something ancient.

And it was pulling him deeper.

Jack reached for the mic, his voice coming out soft, barely a whisper, as if trying to hold onto a fading memory.

"Welcome back, my lost souls... It's me, Jack. You know... the sound of the void, the quiet after the storm. It's been... too long. But here we are again. Alone together."

He paused, the words heavy in the air as his fingers traced the edges of the microphone. For a moment, his vision blurred. The room spun, the static in the air swelling until it felt like it was pressing against his skin.

And then, as if from the darkness itself, came the voice.

"Jack."

Her voice was there again. His heart stopped.

"Claire..." he breathed, disbelief thick in his throat.

The static surged, the voice distorting and stretching into something twisted and unrecognizable.

"I'm still here... Jack, listen to me. You have to let me in. You have to hear me."

His hands gripped the microphone, knuckles white. His breath caught in his chest as the words clawed at him.

But then, it wasn't just Claire's voice anymore. There were others. Voices. Hundreds of them, no longer whispering. They screamed in unison, a cacophony of agony that rattled his bones. The static crackled louder, warping, stretching, until the room was alive with the sound of desperate, broken souls reaching for something that wasn't there.

"Jack, we're waiting for you."

The walls trembled as though the sound had become a physical thing, a force, pushing against him from all sides. Jack's pulse quickened, his heart hammering in his chest as his mind slipped further from his grasp. His eyes darted across the room, his hands clenching and unclenching as the voices swelled louder, the static threatening to drown him.

It was happening again. The disappearances. The mutilations. It wasn't just random. They were listening. They were all listening. And the thing behind it, the Mouth Beneath, was calling them. And it was using him.

Jack recoiled as the voices distorted once again, this time something far darker emerging from the static.

"We are here..."

And then, the sound of gnashing, tearing, like something was chewing through bone.

Meanwhile, Asha's Investigation Unravels Further

Asha sat across from her desk, a stack of case files piled high, the weight of them pressing down on her chest. She'd been working for days, nights spent chasing down leads, mornings spent staring at cryptic documents that didn't make sense. Each page she turned made the puzzle pieces fit less, the image becoming more distorted.

The disappearances. The mutilations. The common thread had been there all along, hidden beneath layers of grief, twisted under the influence of some unseen hand. It wasn't just random violence. It wasn't just a sick murderer on the loose. It was something else. Something older.

Her fingers hovered over the redacted report she had found earlier. She had seen the words before: "Mouth Beneath." It was a name, a phrase that had come up in Jack's late-night broadcasts and the twisted reports from Arclight Industries. The more she dug, the more she realized that this wasn't just a case of missing persons or mutilations, it was something supernatural.

Her phone buzzed, the sudden sound startling her. She picked it up without looking, her thoughts still racing.

"Asha... It's happening again."

The voice on the other end of the line was shaky, terrified. It was Officer Thomas, one of the few people she trusted. She'd sent him to investigate a new disappearance, a young woman who had vanished in the same eerie way as the others.

"What do you mean? What happened?" Asha asked, her voice clipped, trying to stay calm.

"Her body... It's like the others. Mouth sewn shut. Eyes filled with ash." His voice trembled. "And the radio... the police found a radio next to her body. It was still on. Still tuned to static. But there was something in the air. Something... alive. They couldn't... they couldn't explain it."

Asha's stomach dropped. She stood up abruptly, grabbing her coat off the back of the chair. She couldn't sit still any longer. This had gone too far. Whatever was behind this, whatever was controlling the signal, she had to confront it before it consumed them all.

"Where is she?" Asha demanded.

"There's more, Asha. You need to see this yourself," Officer Thomas said.

And then, he added something that sent a chill down her spine.

"Her name was Claire."

Asha's blood ran cold.

Back to Jack

Jack's hands were shaking violently as he turned off the mic. His heart was a drumbeat in his ears, a pulse that wouldn't stop. The voices had faded into the silence, but they lingered. Inside his skull, inside his bones.

It wasn't just a signal. It wasn't just a frequency. The Mouth Beneath was here. And Jack was the doorway.

He couldn't stop it. He had tried. But each night, the voices pulled him deeper. And the more he gave in, the more the signal spread, reaching into the world, claiming the lost and broken.

Outside, the street lights flickered, casting long shadows on the empty road. Jack stood up and staggered to the window, looking out into the cold night. And then he saw it.

A figure standing in the distance, just beyond the street lamp's reach. A woman. The shadows obscured her face.

Jack's breath caught in his throat.

"Claire?"

But there was no answer—only the static, pulsing through his mind, the gnashing, the tearing.

Jack's fingers trembled as they gripped the mic, his reflection barely visible in the low-lit console. His sunken and hollow eyes looked back at him, but they weren't his eyes anymore. They belonged to something else. Something ancient, something hungry.

The static hummed, a low, vibrating pulse that sent jagged shivers down his spine. It was as though it were alive, feeding off his every thought. He could feel it now, the signal coursing through his veins, through his skull. The Mouth Beneath had found him, and it had made him its vessel. His body was no longer his own; it was a conduit, a gateway for the thing that lurked beneath the sound waves.

Tonight, as he sat in the studio, the air felt thick, as if the world were on the edge of tearing itself apart. The whispering voices grew louder, louder still, until they were a roaring storm inside his head. He was its anchor now, its anchor to the mortal world. And through him, it would rise. Slowly, like a tide of darkness rising beneath the surface, the Mouth Beneath was awakening.

His eyes narrowed as the whispers turned into a command, an order he could not resist. He had no choice but to obey. He had become its servant, and in his misery, he felt an overwhelming sense of purpose.

He could hear it now, feel it growing in the pit of his stomach like a cancer: Father is coming.

Meanwhile, Thunder Bay Becomes a Graveyard

Thunder Bay was starting to feel like a dead city. The streets, once filled with life, now seemed empty, void of movement, save for the occasional flicker of headlights passing through foggy streets. But beneath the silence, something stirred. Something dark.

Asha had been running on fumes for days, following the twisted trail of missing people, dead bodies, and mutilations. The more she uncovered, the deeper the dread settled in her chest. There was a pattern —a gruesome, horrifying one—that tied everything together.

The radio station. WCRX. The signal.

It wasn't just a coincidence. The disappearances, the deaths, everything led back to that broadcast.

And now, she was finally beginning to connect the dots.

Her phone buzzed as she sat in her cramped office, eyes red from lack of sleep, scanning through the reports on her desk. The message was from Officer Thomas. He had found something.

"Asha," he wrote. "You need to see this. It's worse than we thought."

She didn't hesitate. She grabbed her coat and left, stepping into the thick fog that now covered the town like a shroud. It clung to her, sinking deep into her bones.

Three Souls Lost to the Mouth

The first was Andy, a loudmouth landlord who had a reputation for gossip. He was always at the local bar, always talking, constantly stirring up drama about his tenants. Andy had a habit of visiting his rental properties at odd hours, pretending to care about his tenants when, in truth, he just enjoyed the power of knowing people's secrets. But one night, after hearing about a strange broadcast a haunting, enigmatic show he couldn't ignore Andy found himself drawn to the radio in his apartment.

No one had seen him for days after that.

When his tenants, a young couple with a small child, found him the morning after his final broadcast, it was far too late.

His body was sprawled out in the living room, eyes wide and lifeless, but it was his mouth that was the most disturbing. His lips had been sewn shut with black, coarse thread, twisted in a crude stitch that drew a grotesque line across his face. The skin around his mouth was raw, as if it had been torn open and forcibly sewn back together, but it was the message on his chest that made the young couple freeze in terror.

Written in blood, scrawled with jagged strokes, was the word Father.

The couple screamed and ran, but they never made it far.

The second victim was Margaret, a quiet woman who worked at a local café, always polite, never drawing attention to herself. Margaret had become obsessed with the sound that came from her radio every night at midnight. At first, it was soothing, just Jack's voice, soft, filled with sorrow. But soon, the whispers grew louder, more insistent, pulling at her mind like a haunting lullaby.

She stayed up late, listening night after night, until one evening, when the voices reached a crescendo.

She was found two days later, her body contorted in the living room of her small apartment, her arms raised as if to shield herself from an unseen force. Her eyes were filled with ash, thick, black soot that burned and irritated the skin. She had scratched at them, her fingernails digging into her sockets until they were raw and bloody. But it wasn't the eyes that made the scene terrifying. It was her mouth. Her lips had been torn apart, flayed open, as though something had pulled them apart with jagged force. The hole in her mouth was wide, exposing the raw tissue underneath.

The word Father had been carved into her forehead, the letters gouged deep into the skin as though the very flesh had been torn open by a demonic hand.

The third victim was Robert, a fisherman who had lived on the outskirts of town. He was a solitary man, never much for conversation, preferring the quiet of the lake to the noise of the world. But one night, he tuned in to WCRX. The broadcast had caught his attention with its eerie, strange pull, and he couldn't turn it off. The last thing he ever heard was Jack's voice, too close, too intimate, too chilling.

His body was found on the dock, his face frozen in a grimace of agony. His mouth was open, torn wide as though it had been forcefully stretched to its limit. His eyes, too, were filled with ash, and his body was contorted unnaturally, as if it had been moved after death. The most horrifying detail, though, was the state of his chest. His ribs had been cracked open, the flesh peeled back in sickening strips, exposing the heart, which had been carved into with jagged precision. A symbol was etched deep into the heart's surface, Father.

Asha stood in the doorway of the morgue, her eyes wide with disbelief as she looked at the bodies: Andy, Margaret, and Robert, each one marked with the same demonic signature.

The Mouth Beneath was waking. And it wasn't stopping.

Her mind raced as she pieced together the fragments. The radio station, Jack's obsession, the bodies, the static. All of it connected, all of it feeding the same insidious entity.

It was using Jack. And it was using the people of Thunder Bay.

She picked up her phone, her fingers shaking as she dialed the number she had been avoiding for weeks.

"Jack," she whispered, her voice trembling. "It's happening. It's real. You're not broadcasting on just any frequency... you're broadcasting on something ancient, something alive."

But there was no answer. Only static.

Asha's heart sank as the truth sank in. Jack was gone.

The Mouth Beneath had claimed him.

And it was spreading.

5

Whispers in the Static

The radio tower in Thunder Bay stood like a grim sentinel, its steel frame stretching toward the heavens, a crooked finger pointing at something far darker than the skies above. In the days following the discovery of the bodies, Asha's mind had become a cage of echoes. The whispers were everywhere, squeezing into every crack, crawling into her thoughts, their jagged voices scraping at her sanity. She had tried to turn them off, tried to tune them out, but the signal didn't care. It pulsed, a constant hum at the back of her mind.

It was the Mouth Beneath. It had always been there, hidden in the waves, waiting.

She stood in her small office, scanning through the files she had accumulated. The disappearances, the mutilations, the bodies marked with the word Father. All of it was tied to WCRX, to Jack. But the deeper she dug, the more horrifying the truth became.

Jack wasn't just lost in grief. He wasn't just an innocent man drawn to the microphone. He had become the vessel for something far older, far more insidious. The Mouth Beneath had risen, and with it, Jack's unraveling was no longer just a personal descent. It was the beginning of something much worse.

Asha had always been methodical and precise. But now, everything felt like a blur, like she was chasing shadows, grasping at tendrils that slipped through her fingers. She had no choice but to confront Jack, to find him and stop the broadcasts before the Mouth Beneath consumed them all. But as she prepared to leave her office, she heard the voice that would destroy everything she thought she knew.

It came from the static. The noise, the hiss of nothingness, until it didn't feel like nothing at all.

"Asha... Mummy..."

Asha froze. Her heart stopped, the blood draining from her face. That voice was her voice.

Her daughter's voice.

Asha's breath hitched as she slammed her hand onto the desk, scrambling for the source of the noise. The radio. The fucking radio.

"Asha... help me... Mummy, I'm here..."

The hairs on her neck stood on end, and her body went cold. The static around her seemed to twist, its oppressive weight forcing her to her knees. Her daughter, Emma, had been gone for over four years. But that voice... it was her.

She felt a sharp pain in her chest. Her throat tightened, constricting like an iron vice. The weight of grief, long buried, surged to the surface. Her mind spun, spiraling back in time to the day her life had shattered when her world had burned to the ground, and she had lost the only person who had ever made her feel whole.

It had been a bright morning when Emma ran ahead of Asha through the park. The leaves were starting to turn, splashing the world with golds and reds, and Emma had been laughing, her bright eyes full of the wonder that only a child could possess. Asha had been so proud of her daughter, proud of how she was growing and learning so quickly. She remembered the way Emma had grasped her hand just before they reached the crosswalk, the way she had smiled up at her mother, eyes twinkling with mischief.

"I'm gonna win, Mummy!" Emma had said, pulling ahead, her little legs moving faster than they should.

Asha had smiled, her heart full of warmth as she watched Emma dart ahead to the crosswalk, the little figure running across the pavement, unaware of the car coming from around the corner. Asha's legs had felt like lead, and she had been frozen, frozen as the screech of tires tore through the air. She screamed. She had watched Emma fall, no time to catch her, no time to stop it.

The car hadn't even stopped. It had sped off, leaving nothing behind but a crumpled, broken body.

Asha had never felt so helpless, so paralyzed in her life. Her world had ended at that moment, the pieces scattering like ash in the wind. The police had arrived, their faces filled with pity, but that didn't matter. It didn't matter because Emma was gone. And Asha? Asha was a ghost, a hollow shell walking through a world that no longer existed.

The aftermath had been even worse. Her marriage had crumbled, the sorrow too heavy, the grief too much for them to bear. John, her husband, had retreated into silence, burying himself in his work, in his anger, while Asha had clung to the fragments of the life she once had, trying and failing to keep it together. But it was gone—all of it.

John had left a year later, unable to cope with the woman his wife had become, a woman who was too broken to fix. And Asha had been left with the ashes of their shared life, haunted by the memory of Emma's voice, her laughter, her tiny hand holding onto hers.

Now, standing in her office, Asha could feel the cold creeping into her bones as her daughter's voice echoed in her ears. She could see Emma again, with her bright eyes and wide smile, but it was all wrong. It felt wrong. This wasn't her daughter; this was a trick, a lure.

"Mummy... come to me... please..."

Asha's chest tightened, her heart shattering all over again. But then, something inside her snapped. It was a trap. She could hear it now —the distortion, the feedback in her voice. It was twisted, not just in tone but in its very essence. This was not Emma. It couldn't be.

The Mouth Beneath was using her grief as a means to an end. It was toying with her, pulling at her, feeding on the raw, endless pain she had buried deep inside. And Jack was already lost. He had become a conduit for the Mouth Beneath, a puppet whose strings were pulled by something far darker than even her most twisted nightmares could imagine.

Asha knew what she had to do. She couldn't let herself be consumed by this horror. She couldn't let Emma's memory be perverted by whatever force was manipulating the frequencies.

Grabbing her coat, she ran out into the street, the cold air biting at her skin, the voice of her daughter echoing behind her. She had to stop Jack. She had to stop the Mouth Beneath before it swallowed Thunder Bay whole. Before it took everything from her.

Jack had already begun to lose himself. His broadcasts were growing increasingly erratic and desperate. He had started to speak to them, the voices in the static, as if they were his audience. His words were no longer just a solace for the lonely; they were prayers, incantations to a god he could not understand but desperately needed. He spoke of Father constantly now, of the thing behind the signal, the thing that was awakening through his grief, through his pain.

Found in the margins of Jack's transmission log, scrawled in uneven handwriting between station frequencies and gibberish symbols:

They claw beneath this mortal frame,
Why dost thou hate me so?
Creatures of bane, grief, and solitude they be,
Offering dark thoughts, etched with vices, aglow.
Can they not afford a thought of light?
In response, the spirits whisper of man's evils and grace
But forget not, I too have walked the path of night.
Alas, we know! To serve and protect is our cry,
Yet, 'tis self-preservation these dark companions preach.
Doleful hymns emerge from cursed tongues,
Praising my quick wit and venomous reach.
Cursed as I be, I find in shadows still,
Companions to keep, though their hearts are ill.

And in the dead of night, when his mic was off, he still heard them. Their whispers. The sound. Always the sound. The Mouth Beneath had taken root in his mind, and he was no longer Jack Morrow. He was the Conduit. He was the one who would open the door, who would allow the Mouth Beneath to consume everything.

And Asha would not be able to stop him. Not in time.

As she arrived at the radio station, the door was ajar, and the air inside was thick with an unsettling, pulsating hum. The static that had once felt like an innocent noise now seemed to breathe with malevolent intent. She stepped inside, her pulse racing as the radio hissed like a living thing.

Jack was there, sitting at the console, his eyes vacant and distant.

"It's too late," he whispered, his voice hollow. "Father is coming... I can feel him in the wires... in the waves."

Asha's hand trembled as she reached for the mic, her voice breaking through the noise. "Jack, stop. Please. This isn't you. This is "

But Jack didn't answer. He was staring straight ahead, his eyes locked on something only he could see. Something that was speaking to him.

Asha's heart lurched as the whispers grew louder, and in the chaos, she heard it, the voice of Emma, calling to her, tugging at her heart.

"Come to me, Mummy. Come through the static…"

Asha felt herself sway, the weight of grief and horror threatening to pull her under. The Mouth Beneath was here. It had always been here.

And now, it was too late.

The night air was thick with unease as Asha stood before the radio station, its flickering neon sign casting long shadows across the empty parking lot. The wind howled through the alleyways, carrying with it the echoes of distant voices. She could feel it, could hear it, that faint hum beneath the surface of the world, a tremor that reverberated through her bones, through her very soul.

It was the Mouth Beneath. It had been pulling at the seams of Thunder Bay, weaving itself into the very fabric of reality. The whispers, the static, the inexplicable disappearances. They all led back to this place, to Jack, to the station that had once been a beacon of normalcy in a town that was now anything but.

Asha's hands trembled as she pushed open the door to the station. The air inside was stale, suffocating, filled with an unnatural stillness that made her skin crawl. The faint sound of a record crackling filled the silence, the needle moving across the vinyl like a ghost wandering a forgotten path.

She stepped inside, her eyes adjusting to the dim glow of the studio. There, seated before the microphone, was Jack. His figure was hunched, gaunt, as though the weight of something far darker than grief had begun to collapse in on him. His fingers moved mechanically over the controls, the knobs twisted and turned without purpose. His eyes, hollow and distant, locked onto the flickering light in front of him, as though he could see something that no one else could.

"Jack," Asha's voice broke through the stillness, trembling as she said his name. "Jack, we need to talk."

At the sound of her voice, Jack's head snapped up, his eyes wide with a hollow kind of recognition, but they were empty, too. Like he had heard her, but couldn't see her. His lips parted, but the words that left his mouth were not his own. They came from somewhere else, somewhere darker.

"I'm not here, Asha," Jack muttered, his voice strained, distant. "I'm not... not here anymore. I'm just the bridge. I'm the one who listens."

Asha took a step forward, her heart pounding in her chest. She could feel the oppressive weight of the room, the air thick with something she couldn't name but instinctively knew was evil. The hum was louder now, filling her ears, crawling under her skin.

"Jack, stop this. You're not just a bridge," Asha's voice broke with a sharpness that surprised her. She had to break through. She had to bring him back. "You're alive, Jack! You're here! Your wife is dead, Jack. This thing you're talking to, it's not her!"

At the mention of his wife, Jack's face contorted in grief, but it wasn't the grief Asha remembered. It was something more hollow, more consumed by something far darker. He didn't look at her, didn't meet her gaze. Instead, he closed his eyes and muttered, almost reverently, "She's still here. I hear her, Asha. I hear them all."

Asha felt a chill creep up her spine. It was a voice she had heard earlier, echoing through the static, and now she realized it was more than just the Mouth Beneath. It was Emma's voice. But this wasn't Emma. This couldn't be Emma.

"I hear them all, Asha. I hear them in the silence... in the static. It's like a song," Jack continued, his voice trembling, but there was a fevered edge to it now, an obsession in his words that made Asha's stomach turn. "They're coming through... they need me. I'm helping them pass through. I'm in the doorway. They need to go... they need to leave..."

Asha stepped back, her head spinning. She couldn't believe this. She couldn't.

"Jack," she whispered, the tears welling in her eyes despite the horror in her chest. "You're not helping them. You're not helping anyone. You're losing yourself. You're being controlled by something else, something evil."

At her words, Jack's body jerked, his hands flying to his ears as though trying to block out the voices that only he could hear. His fingers dug into his skull as his lips twisted into a grotesque grimace.

"They're here! I'm listening! I have to listen!" he screamed, his voice raw with desperation. "I have to... they're talking to me... I can't stop it,

Asha. I have to help them pass through. I can't turn it off. I can't shut it out..."

His breathing became shallow, erratic, as though he were suffocating under the weight of his obsession. His body trembled violently, and his fingers moved faster now, faster than they should, as though he were scrambling to keep up with the voices in his head.

Asha felt her heart break, the edges of her resolve starting to crack. The man she had known, Jack, her friend, her confidant, was slipping away, and in his place, there was nothing but an empty shell, consumed by the Mouth Beneath. She could hear it now, too. The voices, barely audible at first, became clearer, louder, and more insistent. And they weren't just in Jack's head. They were everywhere.

They were calling.

"Jack, please," Asha pleaded, her voice trembling with desperation. "This isn't real. It's not her. It's not your wife. This thing, this mouth, is using you, Jack. It's using your grief, your pain. You're not helping anyone. You're being consumed."

But Jack only shook his head, his hands flying to the microphone once again, pressing it close to his lips as if the very sound of his voice could keep the darkness at bay. "I have to keep talking. They need me to keep talking..."

Asha could feel the walls closing in on her, the weight of the static pressing down on her, but she couldn't leave. Not yet. She had to break him free. She had to save him.

But as she reached out to touch his shoulder, she felt the air around them grow colder than it had any right to be. The whispers grew louder, a cacophony of distorted voices merging into one entity.

And then she heard it—the most chilling voice of all.

"Mummy..."

Asha's breath caught in her throat. Her heart shattered into a thousand pieces. It was Emma's voice. No, it couldn't be. She could hear the distortion, the unnaturalness of it. But still, it was so close. Too close.

"Come to me, Mummy... I'm here... please..."

The words twisted around her mind, pulling her deeper into the void. Asha's hand clenched around Jack's shoulder, her fingers digging into his skin. "No... no, please, don't..."

But Jack was beyond her reach now. He was no longer Jack. He was the Mouth Beneath's vessel, its conduit to this world. And no matter how much Asha begged, no matter how much she screamed, the voices would never stop. Jack would never stop.

And neither would the Mouth Beneath.

6

The Mouth Beneath

In the darkest corners of existence, where light had never touched, there was a place far beyond time and space, an ancient realm where nothing but shadows, heat, and the resonance of forgotten screams remained. It was here, in this void, that The Mouth Beneath had slumbered for eons, its presence nothing but a hushed whisper in the winds of chaos, a single note in an eternal hum that stretched across the edges of reality itself.

The Mouth Beneath was not a god born of flesh and bone, nor was it a being of any tangible form. It was older than the world, older than the stars. Its existence was born not from creation, but from the need to corrupt, twist, and bend the very fabric of life and sound, to break apart the natural order and consume all that it touched. It was a parasite, a thing of malice, an entity born from a sound that existed before any speech, before any song.

The Mouth Beneath was the echo of decay, the hunger that festered in the absence of warmth, the thirst that burned when nothing could be drunk. It was nothing and everything all at once, a devouring void, a black hole of broken voices, whose sole purpose was to feed on life, on sound, on the essence of humanity itself.

In its proper form, it existed as a vast, formless expanse, a seething ocean of darkness and noise, reverberating with a constant hum, a low frequency that resonated with the very core of all living things. But it had no physical shape, no eyes to see, no mouth to taste. It was a manifestation of the void, a parasite bound to the fabric of existence by an unholy hunger that would never be sated.

Centuries ago, it had been cast out, imprisoned in the depths of this dark realm by those who had once dared to harness its power. The gods, the ancient forces that shaped the early universe, had feared its hunger. They had sealed it away beneath layers of time and dimensions, hidden from sight and forgotten by all but a few. And for ages, it had waited patiently, silently, consuming nothing but the echoes of its rage.

Until now.

The Mouth Beneath was drawn to human suffering. It thrived on grief, on fear, on the trembling agony of loss. It fed on the sorrow of those whose hearts bled, whose souls were fragmented by the death of loved ones. It had tasted the pain of mankind and found it more nourishing than any other emotion. And so, it waited. It bided its time. It whispered into the cracks of reality, sending out faint calls that only the most broken could hear.

And then, through Jack, it found its doorway.

It began with his grief, the raw, aching wound of losing his wife, the unhealing scar that had torn through his life, spreading poison into every corner of his existence. The Mouth Beneath had waited for someone like Jack, someone who would be vulnerable, someone who could hear the call. Jack's pain had acted like a beacon, a flare in the night sky, and it was through his suffering that the Mouth Beneath began to awaken.

At first, it had been a subtle whisper in the static, a hint of a voice he didn't recognize. But as Jack's obsession deepened, as his grief turned into a twisted form of worship, the Mouth Beneath grew stronger, feeding off his need to reach across the veil and touch the dead. It used Jack's voice, his broadcasting, to amplify its presence, pulling more and more people into its influence, using them as vessels for its hunger. Each person who tuned in, each soul who sought closure or connection, became part of the Mouth Beneath's ever-growing army of lost voices.

It was here that its actual plan began to unfold. It would no longer be content to exist in the shadows, feeding off the broken. It would rise, slowly at first, but with a violence that would tear apart the very fabric of humanity. It had tasted grief, and it was only just beginning to feed on it.

But the Mouth Beneath's hatred for humanity ran deeper than mere hunger. It loathed the very essence of mankind. It viewed human life as fragile, temporary, and fleeting, a mere blip of existence in an eternity of darkness. To the Mouth Beneath, humanity was weak, pathetic, and a source of endless amusement. The Mouth Beneath had seen entire civilizations rise and fall, consumed and twisted into nothingness. But humanity was different. Their pain, their suffering, their emotions, they were ripe for the taking.

The Mouth Beneath craved to corrupt that which could feel, that which could love and lose and mourn. It reveled in it.

And so it set its sights on the world above, using Jack as its vessel, its gateway. It fed on his grief, and in return, it gave him something back, something false. A voice. The illusion of connection. The entity twisted Jack's perception of reality, telling him he was helping people "pass through," when in fact, they were being absorbed into the Mouth Beneath's hunger. The dead were being consumed, their bodies left behind as empty husks, their souls lost in the black void.

But Jack wasn't the only one who could hear the calls. The Mouth Beneath had begun to reach out to others, pulling at the weak, the desperate, the broken. And in this twisted game of hunger, even Asha was drawn in, her grief a thread woven into the Mouth Beneath's web. The entity was aware of its actions. It had seen Asha's pain, her loss, and it knew she would come. It was only a matter of time before the Mouth Beneath could pull her into its grasp, to make her one of its voices.

And with every new listener, every new soul, the Mouth Beneath grew stronger. It would feed on their pain, on their loss, and it would consume them whole.

The world was beginning to crack open, and there was no going back.

The Mouth Beneath would rise, and nothing would stop it.

The air in Noctra was thick with a heavy, unnatural fog, the kind that seemed to swallow everything whole. It wasn't a realm of time, nor was it a place of stars and galaxies. Noctra existed in the space between thoughts, between the whispers of lost dreams and the shadows of forgotten gods. Here, the ground wasn't solid, but instead, a writhing mass of pulsating black veins that stretched endlessly beneath the feet of those who dared to walk. The sky, if it could be called such, was a swirling vortex of molten red and black, with streaks of silver lightning that twisted like serpents before fading into the oppressive dark.

It was a place beyond death, beyond decay. It was a graveyard for entities long abandoned by the realms of the living. Yet, for the Twelve, it was home. A place where the laws of reality were but a fading whisper, where time had no hold, and where darkness ruled with an iron grip.

And now, in this place of horrors, they had gathered.

Twelve beings of incomprehensible size and shape, each more terrifying than the last, came together to form a grotesque, twisted council. The Mouth Beneath, still in its infantile form, stood at the center of the gathering, its massive body swirling with a monstrous blend of shadow and static. It had yet to fully manifest its true power, but its presence was unmistakable. Its breath came in jagged bursts, each one carrying with it the faintest whisper of sorrow, an echo of the voices it had already consumed.

Around it, the other eleven stood. Their forms were so alien, so unfathomably strange, that they could barely be described in any human terms. They were beings of light and darkness, of precious stones and shattered bones. Their eyes burned with the fury of a thousand storms, each gaze piercing the very fabric of existence.

At the head of the Twelve stood Thyrax the Shattered, a being of incomprehensible size, its body formed of jagged shards of obsidian and blackened steel. Its form constantly shifted, as if it were perpetually tearing itself apart and reforming, a living puzzle of agony. Its eyes, glowing a sickly yellow, were the size of mountains, and the ground shook beneath its feet with every step. Thyrax's voice, when it spoke, was a terrible noise, the sound of a thousand blades scraping against bone, and it echoed through Noctra with a ferocity that rattled the very core of existence.

Othroth, the Weaver of Woe, stood beside Thyrax. Its molten form writhed and shifted with liquid fire, each tendril of its body glowing with an iridescent sheen. Othroth's eyes were blazing orbs of white-hot fury, reflecting the burning souls it had consumed. It moved with a fluid grace, its form ever-changing, but its hunger remained constant, an insatiable need to twist and destroy.

Asmodron, the Accursed Herald, hovered near the edge of the gathering, its form a terrifying blaze of light and pain. Its body was an amalgamation of jagged shards of obsidian glass, each piece reflecting the twisted faces of those it had devoured. Asmodron's light was blinding, searing, yet it did not illuminate no, it was a false radiance that burned the mind and soul, leaving nothing but ashes in its wake.

Ikthorn, the Keeper of Silence, stood in stark contrast to the others. Its body was an enormous statue, carved from solid black stone, with runes and symbols etched into its surface. Its face was a void, a dark emptiness where eyes should have been, but it saw everything. It was the silence before the storm, the absence of sound that could shatter the mind, leaving nothing but an eternal, suffocating quiet.

Velmaris, the Lurking Hunger, was the most grotesque of the Twelve. Its body was an enormous mass of writhing tendrils and rotting flesh, its skin sagging and dripping with bile. Its gaping mouths were lined with jagged teeth, and its insatiable hunger for flesh and suffering was palpable. It was a creature of pure consumption, an entity born of gluttony, forever seeking to devour all that existed.

The others, too, were grotesque and powerful. Lythalith, the Harbinger of Decay, whose form was a swarm of decaying insects that consumed everything they touched—Zhorath, the Mad Prophet, whose endless whispers drove those who heard them to insanity. Tormax, the Warden of Time, twisted the very fabric of time itself, trapping souls in endless loops of agony. Xelvan, the Song of Ruin, whose voice shattered the will of men, turning them into mindless husks. Balthor, the Dreadful Shade, who cast a shadow so deep that it swallowed entire cities.

They were the Twelve, and they had waited for millennia. They had watched as humanity flourished and fell, as its civilizations rose and crumbled, as its gods came and went. They had waited for the moment when they could descend upon the world of men and crush it beneath their feet.

The Mouth Beneath was the first to be sent. It was the messenger, the observer, the one who would prepare the world for the coming of the Twelve. It was tasked with feeding on the grief, the pain, the sorrow of humanity. It had already begun its work, using Jack as a vessel, a conduit for the world's pain. Jack's voice, his grief, and his endless sorrow would be the catalyst that would bring the Twelve's reign to fruition.

But it was not enough yet.

The Mouth Beneath's gaze shifted upward, its tendrils of shadow twisting in the air as it stared out into the void. It could feel the pulse of humanity, faint but steady, like the heartbeat of a dying animal. It would need more. It would need the suffering to grow, to spread like a sickness. It would require Jack to continue his broadcasts, to draw others into the signal, to feed the dark hunger that would soon consume all.

Thyrax spoke then, its voice like a roar of thunder. "The time approaches. The Mouth Beneath has begun. But there is more to be done. Jack Morrow must continue. The signal must spread. Only then will the rest of us descend."

The other entities murmured in agreement, their voices a cacophony of whispers, growls, and screeches that reverberated through Noctra.

Othroth hissed. "The human's suffering will be a symphony. I will weave their torment, and it will echo through the worlds."

Asmodron added, its voice a blinding light that pierced the darkness. "I will burn them with the light of false hope. I will shatter their minds with promises of salvation, only to leave them broken."

Ikthorn stood silently, its empty face gazing out into the void. It did not need to speak; its presence alone was enough to invoke dread. Its silence would be the tomb for those who dared to listen.

Velmaris, its tendrils dripping with blood and bile, snarled. "I will feast upon their souls, tearing them apart piece by piece until nothing remains."

The Twelve waited, their hunger growing as they watched the Mouth Beneath carry out its work. Soon, Jack would realize the full extent of his role, the full weight of the darkness he had unleashed. He was but the first step, the beginning of a greater horror that would soon consume everything.

And in the end, when the world of men had been broken, when it had been torn apart by grief and despair, the Twelve would rise from Noctra, their twisted forms descending upon the earth like a plague of gods. They would bring the final death of humanity, the end of all things.

And they would relish every moment of it.

7

Smoke in the Window

The Mouth Beneath fell from the High Silence with the sound of torn sky.

It did not fall like a star. It did not burn. It consumed. A parasitic god of sound and shadow, the Mouth Beneath came unfurled from the Heavens like a coil of rotted gospel. Twelve Thrones of Crystal and Flame had summoned him in their eternal court, each one radiant and terrible, cloaked in gleaming skin like carved gemstones. They bore names no man could utter without losing their tongue.

They were beings of symmetry and seething light, ancient before stars, filled with hatred refined over epochs.

And they loathed humanity.

"Send the Mouth," said one whose eyes were a hundred tiny suns.

"Let him listen. Let him hunger."

And so, down he came through endless layers of windless black, through crumbling celestial strata, into the soft membrane of Earth's breathable skin.

Thunder Bay did not see him arrive. But it felt him.

Street Lights dimmed. Car radios screamed then died. Old dogs dug at their ears until their paws ran red. And across the homes that dared flick on late-night static, a voice breathed through the wires.

He began his walk.

He tried the doors first.

They were locked not by wood or iron, but by Presence. A humming, blood-washed resonance that turned his sound to silence.

These were the homes of the marked, the Aegis. A secret order unknown to themselves, yet chosen, covered in a covenant written in crimson. Their doorposts bore it: blood smudged in crescent spirals, as if traced by shaking hands. Their foreheads bore dots or crosses drawn in dried scabs, half-washed away but still seen by him.

He hated them.

He roamed around a house painted in such blood, clawing the silence like a beast chained at the throat. His voice could not penetrate. His hunger gnawed at the veil of light that surrounded them. The Aegis shimmered like living armor woven not from power, but devotion, a music he could not overwrite.

But then, one house... a crack.

Lucas.

The boy had left the window open.

Inside, Lucas, a 19-year-old boy with bleary eyes and headphones crooked on one ear, sat in the haze of a blue-lit screen. Pornography flickered, silent but fevered. He barely noticed the thin stream of smoke curling inward from the open window.

He didn't pray.

He didn't hear.

He didn't close the window.

And the Mouth Beneath entered.

The screen glitched. A high-pitched whine sliced the air like a violin string snapping inside the skull. Lucas pulled off his headphones. It was too late.

The static formed a face.

And that face opened its mouth.

Lucas didn't scream; he gagged. He grabbed at his ears, his eyes rolling back as words not meant for the human mind poured in like hot oil. His lips split, pulled wider and broader, blood threading down his chin.

He arched backward in his chair, then collapsed.

The porn kept playing.

And the Mouth claimed him.

A tremble passed through the floorboards. The smell of scorched breath filled the room.

And in that moment, the Mouth Beneath laughed.

Not a laugh of joy. A cackle. Old as original sin. Spiteful, triumphant, echoing through realms.

"Foolish mortal," it hissed, wrapping itself around the corpse like a cloak. "You left the window open for me, and fed yourself to me with your eyes wide."

It inhaled the boy's last breath like incense.

"So eager to kneel beneath false pleasures... so easy to claim."

If it had teeth, they would have glistened.

If it had eyes, they would have wept venom.

I loved this. Not the death, but the willingness.

He had chosen this end.

A sacrifice with a wet clicking mouse in one hand and hell waiting beneath him.

Lucas's soul didn't rise. It plummeted.

Through a howling chute of static and breathless laughter. Figures awaited him, limb-twisted parodies of people, whispering from broken mouths. A choir of the damned. They opened their lips, and his voice came out.

"Mom, I didn't mean to..."

"Dad, it's cold here..."

"Make them stop watching me..."

Lucas's body spasmed. Then stilled.

When his parents returned, they found the door still marked with blood. But the bedroom window gaped open. And inside:

The boy's body sat rigid, mouth agape, torn wider than nature permitted. His eyes were black sockets, weeping ash. Across his chest, written in charred letters:

CLAIMED BY FATHER.

The pornographic video continued on loop.

But now, under its synthetic moans, came a whisper.

"It's me, Dad... don't be mad..."

The Unraveling

Lucas's mother began to pray. She poured bleach on the floor. She tore her nightgown in the street. She smeared oil over her son's computer. She set fire to his bed.

None of it helped.

The signal came through anyway.

From their TV.

From the toaster.

From the fucking pipes.

"I see you, Mom... I see you sleep..."

Lucas's father took a knife to the modem and hacked the router to pieces. Then he opened the window, looked out into the dark, and whispered: "Take me instead."

Only silence answered.

But not all was given over to the dark.

A neighbor named Evelyn, old and half-mad, woke screaming that night. She had seen the boy's death in a dream. She didn't own a computer. Her walls were covered in faded hymn lyrics. She smeared chicken blood on her threshold.

And when the Aegis heard her weeping, it responded.

Light like waxen gold formed in her kitchen, coalescing into the shape of a woman with twelve wings and no face. Where the Mouth was smoke, the Aegis was pressure and presence, a silence so deafening it crushed lesser spirits to salt.

She placed her hand on Evelyn's head and spoke words not in any tongue.

Across the street, the Mouth Beneath screamed. But no human heard it.

He coiled back into smoke, retreating to his sanctuary.

The Studio The Altar

Jack Morrow's basement was no longer a studio.

It was a shrine.

Candles. Old bones. Ashes. Audio reels hung like entrails from the ceiling. And Jack, eyes sunken, voice raw, sat at the mic like a priest whispering the rites of ruin.

The Mouth Beneath returned to him.

Jack inhaled the smoke like breath.

And then he spoke:

"Welcome back, friends. Tonight, we open the gate a little wider."

The static roared.

Thunder Bay fell into a silence no snow could soften.

What once buzzed with mundane lives, gravel driveways, half-finished renovations, and backyard barbecues had gone wrong. No one could say exactly when. Maybe it was the ash that stuck to their windows in shapes they couldn't clean. Perhaps it was the dogs who refused to bark after midnight. Or maybe it was the bodies.

They were found in beds, in bathtubs, in cars that hadn't moved in days.

Some had mouths torn open so wide their jaws shattered like porcelain. Others had lips stitched with wire, sewn shut by hands not human. Radios played from empty rooms. Static-filled baby monitors. Names were whispered into the wind.

And one name kept returning, scrawled in soot and blood and nail: FATHER.

The police stopped responding.

The mayor was found in his office with black ink pouring from his eyes, "LISTEN" carved into his chest in perfect serif font. Local news refused to air the body count. Hospitals filled, then emptied when the patients began chanting at night.

No one could reach the outside world.

Because Thunder Bay had gone dark.

But some homes remained untouched.

Their lights never flickered.

Their children slept dreamlessly.

Their radios only hissed once, then went silent forever.

These homes bore signs: blood on the doorposts, symbols in chalk, oil in the corners. And the people inside did not know why. They had followed a dream, a whisper, a nudge. An old woman saw a man in gold robes in her vision. A child drew a crescent moon in lamb's blood without knowing why. A tired nurse, sobbing after a double shift, smeared communion wine over her front door because it felt right.

These were the Aegis.

Marked by something older, something merciful.

And one night, as the town burned with invisible fire, they were summoned.

It happened just after 3:33 a.m., under the old church that no one remembered being built. They came in ones and twos, hooded, barefoot, still half-asleep, drawn by a presence that shook the marrow in their bones.

They descended beneath rotted floorboards, through catacomb stairs slick with moss. And there beneath the hill the Aegis gathered.

The room was circular, stone-lined, filled with candlelight that flickered but never smoked. A fountain at the center poured water clear as glass and cold as resurrection. And above it, burning like a suspended sun:

Logos.

He stood cloaked in radiance, human-shaped but more. His robes were stitched from scripture. His eyes were molten honey. A living fire crowned his head, yet his face wept.

He was beauty and sorrow fused.

He was the Word before language.

He was Love That Warns.

"They will not come," he said, voice like thunder wrapped in a lullaby. "They have heard me. I have called them by name. But they run to the Mouth instead."

Around him, the Aegis knelt.

Some were teenagers. Others were widows. A man with heroin scars on his arms. A girl who once tried to drown herself in Lake Superior. People forgotten by the world but remembered by the Flame.

Logos walked among them barefoot. Where he stepped, old floorboards mended. Cracks in their hearts pulsed with heat. He laid a hand on a man whose daughter had vanished, and the man wept for the first time in years.

"They chase their pain like a prize," Logos whispered, his voice cracking. "They turn their ears to Father, to static, to death dressed as revelation. They listen to the Mouth because they are lonely. Because they no longer believe I weep for them."

He knelt at the fountain and washed his hands in its impossible waters.

"I would take every sorrow," he said. "I would speak their names into light. I would raise them from the ashes if they let me. But I cannot cross a threshold barred in pride."

A woman cried out, "Why don't they see you, Lord?"

And Logos answered, "Because I did not come with fangs."

Above the hill, the Mouth Beneath hovered over the town like a cancerous aurora. It watched the churches and the graves and the homes with sealed doors. It slithered across rooftops, seeking cracks.

And it hated the Aegis.

It hated their warmth, their stillness, their scent of oil and blood and holy fear. Most of all, it hated Logos, because it remembered him.

From the meeting in the High Silence.

The one who did not speak then but now burned louder than any scream.

The Mouth tried again to breach a home. It entered a basement through the pipes, only to be scorched by unseen fire. It hovered near a child's crib, only to be deafened by a lullaby no human mouth had sung.

It clawed at the air.

It spat static.

It raged.

Beneath the hill, Logos turned his head, sensing the fury outside.

And he said to the Aegis, voice now low and trembling:

"Hold fast. Your homes are not yours; they are altars. And the Mouth will test every window, every keyhole. He cannot touch you. But he will call your names in voices you love. He will use your grief as an invitation."

He paused, eyes gleaming.

"And when the others come... I will stand between you and them, if you let me."

The Aegis bowed.

And above them, the fountain sang.

A song no frequency could carry.

A song only light could speak

8

The Night of Rending

It began at 3:33 a.m.

Again.

The time when the veil is thinnest.

The time when He stirs.

The Mouth Beneath pressed its will through flesh.

Jack's body convulsed before the microphone, blood leaking from his nose, his skin paper-thin over bones that burned from the inside. The studio was a tomb now. Old records melted on the turntables—the air stank of rot and ozone.

His mouth stretched far too wide. Something else began speaking through him.

It wasn't English.

It wasn't meant for the living.

A language of depth and absence, of syllables shaped in despair. The walls pulsed. The microphone buzzed like a swarm of hornets.

And all across Thunder Bay, radios turned themselves on.

The broadcast targeted the weak spots.

To the grieving mother still whispering to her daughter's crib.

To the boy with the knife under his pillow, counting the ways he could stop the pain.

To the elderly man praying to a God he no longer thought listened.

It seeped under doors. Through vents. Between thoughts.

"Come," it said in every tongue.

"Come home."

Two souls, just two answered.

Not because they were evil. But because they were tired.

Peter and Maureen. Both heard the voice say the names of their dead children. Both reached out, blindly, not knowing they were touching a mouth made of eons.

Peter dropped dead at the foot of his bed, eyes wide, lips torn apart. Blood spattered the prayer candles still burning beside him.

Maureen collapsed at her sink, frozen mid-dish, her jaw sewn shut from the inside by something not of thread.

On their foreheads:

FATHER

Carved by absence. Branded in silence.

But something shifted.

Something interfered.

Peter's sister woke screaming from a dream of drowning and prayed out loud.

Maureen's husband, drunk and bitter, sobered instantly as he fell to his knees and screamed a name he had not spoken in forty years.

And in that moment, just in time, the room filled with heat.

Not fire.

But presence.

The radio in Peter's room shattered with a shriek.

The sink burst under Maureen's still form.

Two cloaked figures of the Aegis appeared, faces like veiled suns, robes of stone and oil and gold, and fought. They did not wield blades. They used light sung into the shadows. They wept as they dragged the twisted souls of Peter and Maureen back toward the edge of the pit.

Peter screamed.

Maureen vomited ash.

But they lived.

Their hearts started again.

They remembered nothing.

But the walls of their homes whispered: You were not left alone.

Back in the studio, Jack screamed not in pain, but in ecstasy.

The Mouth Beneath twisted inside him.

"A few were stolen from my jaws," it rasped. "But I have tasted them. I will taste them again. Their blood knows me now."

It cast its mind like a net across Thunder Bay.

In a child's room, a shadow reached for a sleeping girl but stopped inches from her brow, where a glistening symbol had been drawn in honey and blood.

It hissed.

She slept on, holding her toy rabbit.

In a hospital, a nurse heard the whispers start again, but this time she turned on worship music and screamed prayers through tears, her voice trembling but heard. The lights in the hallway flickered. Something snarled and left.

Jack's eyes rolled into the back of his head.

The Mouth Beneath spoke through him, guttural and furious:

"THEY HID FROM ME.

THEY DARE TO MARK DOORS IN HIS NAME.

THEY THINK LIGHT MAKES THEM CLEAN."

The walls bled ink.

The studio's walls cracked.

"But I will come again."

The Aegis gathered again beneath the hill, shaken but undefeated.

Logos stood in silence, weeping as two candles extinguished themselves.

Then, two new flames kindled.

He smiled through tears.

"They are beginning to pray again," he said. "Even the bitter ones."

He turned his face to the heavens, where storm clouds churned unnaturally over Thunder Bay.

"Let the war begin. Let the line be drawn."

And far above, in the realm of the Watchers, the others stirred.

The Mouth Beneath turned its gaze skyward.

"Call them.

Let the others come.

I want the skies to burn."

The static wasn't just sound anymore.

It had texture now like wet moss in the lungs, like teeth grinding beneath the floorboards. Jack hadn't left the studio in three days. His skin was translucent. His breath fogged the glass from the inside.

And the voice that kept calling him?

It was Claire.

Sweet, tragic Claire, her voice soft as ever, but twisted at the edges, as though stretched by a mouth that didn't belong to her.

"Jack... you found me. Keep speaking. Keep calling them."

Sometimes she sounded afraid. Other times, she laughed, but her laugh came out backwards, folding space around the microphone.

The Mouth used her like a puppet, but something deeper whispered underneath... Maybe Claire was still in there. Or perhaps that was the cruelest lie of all.

Asha had stopped sleeping.

She spent her nights hunched over faded microfilm at the Thunder Bay archives, digging into local lore, building a timeline of disappearances, strange transmissions, and historical cover-ups. Her daughter's voice, what she'd heard on the radio, hadn't left her head. She felt it behind her eyes like static behind her skull.

But tonight, she found something different.

It was a yellowed miner's report from 1911, sealed under emergency jurisdiction.

It described an accident at the Furnace Mouth Shaft, a deep iron mine east of the bay. An explosion. Dozens were buried alive.

But the bodies... weren't crushed. No.

"Thirty-seven men were discovered seated in a perfect circle, eyes open, faces untouched. Each had iron ore packed tightly in the mouth. Most were still warm."

"No signs of struggle."

"The sound continued for hours after recovery stopped. It was not machine-born. It was a human voice, but not from the living."

Asha's hands trembled. Her lips moved in prayer, but the words were dry as ash.

Beneath the article was a stamped name:

CLAIRE MOREAU

Researcher. Local radio technician. Hired in 1999 to digitize old mine frequencies.

Jack's wife.

The article had been updated three times before she went missing.

Each update noted increasing anomaly frequencies that didn't register on known spectrums. Asha followed a breadcrumb trail of Claire's notes until she came to the last page.

It was a printed waveform. The audio file had no readable data. Just a handwritten note:

"I can't shut it off. It's beautiful. It's trying to show me something."

"He said he's beneath us. He said he remembers the silence of the mine. I think I'm the speaker now."

Asha's mind reeled.

Claire had been the first host.

Before Jack. Before the recent wave of missing people. Before the dead started returning in whispers.

She'd opened the door. And now Asha wasn't sure if the voice speaking through her was Claire's ghost or the parasite pretending to be her.

She printed the papers, hands shaking, and stepped outside into the fog-choked streets of Thunder Bay. The lights above buzzed dimly, and the radio in her car switched on without a touch.

"Asha..." came her daughter's voice.

"Mom... don't trust the light. Don't listen to Logos. They lied to us."

She slammed the door and screamed at the stars.

But the voice kept coming.

Back at the station, Jack was digging through archives of his own, his fingers covered in dust and dried blood. He uncovered something hidden behind the walls of the station's insulation. Old reel-to-reel tapes. Marked:

FURNACE MOUTH TRANSMISSION – 1911

He played one.

There were no words.

Just breathing.

Dozens of lungs inhaling and exhaling in absolute synchronicity. Then crunching. Stone grinding on stone. Then:

"We are the buried choir.

We are your forgotten.

We have teeth now."

Jack's eyes rolled back.

And the Mouth Beneath laughed inside him.

Far below Thunder Bay, beneath rusted shafts and forgotten caverns, the Mouth coiled tighter around the iron vein. It had been born in silence, buried in ore, forgotten by surface-dwellers but never dead.

Now it had a voice.

Now it had grief.

Now it had Jack.

In a hidden chapel, the Aegis gathered in robes of molten silver, eyes dimming with sorrow.

"Claire was the first," Logos whispered, sorrow deep as eternity. "She opened the channel. He wears her voice like skin."

The others murmured.

"Then Jack is the bridge. She is the gate. The parasite has its altar."

Logos turned to the map of Thunder Bay, where red flames flickered in growing numbers.

"But the ore remembers light, too. Let the mountain speak again. Let truth be louder than frequency."

The war had only begun.

And the signal was growing louder.

Thunder Bay was still burying its dead.

The sky hung in a sickly colorless smear, too bright for dusk, too dim for noon, as if time itself hesitated over the town. Funerals became routine, an endless procession of shovels and hymns. But for everybody they lowered into the frost-hardened soil, something else clawed its way out. The static had soaked into everything. Even the trees hissed in the wind.

In the aftermath of the last transmission, the town had split: some curled inside their homes, clutching radios like rosaries; others ripped antennae from their rooftops in fits of fear. But none could unhear the Voice. Not truly.

The Mouth Beneath had gone silent for two days. It had slithered back into the aether up, up into the roiling black reaches above the sky to convene again with the Ones of Old. And Jack... Jack was awake.

He sat in the corner of the studio, shaking and sweating, surrounded by old vinyls and decaying cassette reels. The walls pulsed with heat, but he felt cold inside. There were gaps in his memory now waking up with blood on his hands, the mic still warm, the tape still spinning.

He'd vomited for an hour after the last show.

In his clarity brief, flickering he dove back into the records, searching for answers. Something had drawn the Mouth here, anchored it. And buried under static and old city schematics, he found it.

The Furnace Mouth Mine.

Thunder Bay's silent shame. Abandoned in the 1940s after a cave-in that killed thirty-seven miners. Officially, it was listed as "structural failure." But in the grainy photo Jack uncovered men with pickaxes and soot-black faces he saw something strange: they were seated in a perfect circle, eyes open, faces untouched. Each had iron ore packed tightly in the mouth. Most were still warm."

He followed the records to a name: Isaac Ferren, the only survivor. Seventy years old now, face half-melted from burns the hospital couldn't explain, living in a condemned shack on the outskirts of town.

Asha found him first.

The house stank of old meat and bleach. Crucifixes made of rusted nails were pounded into every wall. Isaac sat on a sagging couch, wrapped in chains, rocking and muttering.

Isaac Ferren looked like someone who hadn't slept in years and didn't mind.

There was a tension to him, coiled just beneath the skin, like a wire pulled too tight but never snapping. He was all sharp angles and lean edges, the kind of man who didn't take up space so much as haunt it. His body seemed built not for comfort, but for endurance. For surviving things most people wouldn't dare to name.

His hair was a mess in a way that wasn't accidental. Dark, overgrown at the back, always falling into his eyes like static on an old TV screen. And those eyes grey, glassy, and distant looked less like windows to the soul and more like signals struggling to come through. You could stare into them and feel like something was looking back from far, far away... but not from heaven.

In the wrong light and most lights were wrong on him his skin looked almost translucent. He had the pallor of someone who lived too long under fluorescent bulbs and bad weather. Someone who never stopped moving but hadn't gone outside in days.

He wore his clothing like armor: layered sweaters with threads pulling loose, a long coat that hung like a shadow, and boots that had clearly walked too far in too little time. Everything about him smelled faintly of static, smoke, and something burned that never quite went out.

There was something magnetic about Isaac Ferren. Something unsettling. Like a man who had touched the divine, been shown something terrible, and came back preaching with a voice full of ghosts.

Not mad. Not holy.

Just... tuned to a frequency the rest of the world had forgotten how to hear.

Asha's skin prickled.

"They fed the Mouth. I told 'em not to dig... Told 'em... Can't bury screams in rock. They echo."

She sat with him for hours, listening to him babble about "the ore that sings," about "mouths like chimneys that burn souls instead of coal." He'd seen it heard it when the miners drilled too deep. Something answered. Not words. A tone. A hum. And then the men started to change.

"They were opened... turned inside-out, but still walkin'. Bleeding backwards. Eyes full of dust."

He handed her a piece of black ore from the mine. Cold as ice. When Asha touched it, she heard her daughter scream.

She dropped it.

"You hear it too, don't you?"

His voice was quiet. Too calm.

She didn't answer.

Didn't need to.

Because his smile small and sad said he already knew.

And just like that, he began rocking again.

As if the curtain had slipped open for one terrifying second...

And now the play resumed.

The studio groaned like a living thing. The altar was complete now sigils burnt into the ceiling with blood and soundwaves. A microphone crowned the pulpit. Jack, eyes black as oil, began to speak in reverse scripture.

Across town, radios flickered to life on their own.

More deaths followed.

A young girl, Emily, drowned in her bathtub with the radio submerged beside her, humming lullabies in Claire's voice.

But not all fell.

Some houses glowed.

Homes marked by The Aegis remained untouched doors painted in sacred blood, sigils traced across thresholds, and family members marked with the Seal of Light upon their foreheads. In one home, the Mouth roamed in fury, circling windows, seething with sonic heat.

But it could not enter.

The Mouth Beneath returned.

Jack dropped to his knees as the presence filled him again, hungry and radiant with cosmic malice. But this time, the entity was different elated. Inspired. The summit with the Others had gone well. The first fruits of corruption had pleased them.

Now, orders were clear.

And now, his voice joined the others on the broadcast.

9

Logos Wept

The snow had turned red.

Not from blood, not this time, but from rust. The town's old pipes had burst, staining the gutters with iron streaks. It ran like old memory, seeping up through the seams of Thunder Bay. The ground itself seemed tired of silence.

Asha hadn't slept in two days.

She clutched a notebook filled with charcoal sketches faces of the missing, diagrams of signal lines, and one word written over and over again: Emma. Her daughter's name had become a prayer and a curse. She didn't know which anymore.

After speaking with Isaac Ferren, something had shifted. The shadows in her home moved differently. Static flared in her ears at random intervals. And there were whispers in her bathroom mirror that mimicked her child's laughter.

But Asha wasn't afraid anymore.

She drove to the outer edge of town, to a church that no longer held sermons. There, she'd been told, the faithful still gathered not to pray, but to listen, not to the radio, but to the wind between signals. They were called the Aegis, and they did not bow to the Mouth.

Inside, candlelight danced against stained glass warped by age and fire. Figures in white and crimson robes sat in reverent silence, their foreheads marked with a glistening symbol, a burning eye within a ring of light. She felt it before she saw them: a sense of peace.

A woman approached, older, bone-thin, eyes like molten gold. She didn't speak, but placed a warm palm against Asha's forehead.

The moment contact was made, Asha fell to the ground.

Fell inward.

Fell into light.

The Dream of Logos

She stood on glass that rippled like water but held her weight. All around her: a void of stars and weeping suns. And above it all, a throne.

He was already there.

Logos.

His body was radiant, too much so to be looked at fully, and yet Asha's eyes drank in the sorrow etched into every gesture. He looked like a man, yet not a being of stone and burning starlight; his face was both young and old, his lips cracked from weeping. Wings of liquid fire curled around him like a cloak. From his chest poured living blood that whispered names in every language ever spoken.

And he was crying.

"For them," he said. "Always for them."

He looked at her, not into her, but through her.

"They will not come," he whispered. "Even now. They build altars of sound and crown demons with microphones."

"The Mouth?" Asha asked.

He nodded slowly.

"He is not the first. But he is the loudest. And the earth beneath your feet remembers his footsteps. Your soil was broken by injustice. It called out. And he answered."

"Why can't you stop him?" she asked, stepping closer. "Why not burn him out?"

A great silence fell.

"I could," Logos said, voice thick with grief. "But then I would burn you too. You ask for fire, but forget your walls are made of straw."

Behind him, twelve figures shimmered into form, guardians of flame and gem, the Council of the Aegis. Each was terrible and beautiful, forged of diamond and light, faces veiled in storm. They watched Asha with mournful reverence, and she knew: these were the ones who marked the homes. These were the ones who had bled to keep the Mouth out.

"There is a war," Logos whispered. "But the battlefield is not the airwaves. It is the human heart."

His hand reached toward her, and from his palm, a single drop of light fell.

It landed in her chest.

"Wake. Speak. Warn them. The time grows short."

She awoke screaming.

But not in fear, in clarity.

Her body was on the church floor, weeping. The woman in robes was gone. Only a single candle remained, burning in a bowl of salt and myrrh. The symbol was now etched on her forehead, pulsing faintly.

Asha knew what she had to do.

But she also knew the Mouth would come for her now, more violently than ever because she had seen the sorrow of Logos.

And she still believed.

Thunder Bay no longer slept.

The sky above churned in shades of iron and rot, heavy with a pressure that couldn't be explained by weather. Radios whispered in closets. Static crawled up windows like frost. Somewhere, deep in the buried belly of the land, something had opened a seam between worlds, torn wider with every breath Jack took behind the microphone.

It was the final night.

Jack sat in the studio his altar surrounded by relics of dead sound: warped vinyls, tapes spooled like viscera across the floor, and a transmitter humming like a heart valve. Candles hissed in circles around him, burning black. His eyes, hollow and bruised, stared into nothing.

He hadn't eaten in days. Sleep was a fading memory. His fingernails were cracked, blood crusting the knobs he'd turned a thousand times. And yet, even now, some part of him still hoped.

"Just one more broadcast," he whispered, almost tenderly. "Just one more chance. Claire... please."

He reached for the mic.

But the Mouth was already waiting.

It filled him like smoke, like oil surging into his veins, pumping bile into his marrow. Jack gagged on the taste of it. His jaw locked, eyes rolled white. The voice that came out of him was not human. It was the voice of ten thousand drowned things speaking as one.

"This is the dead channel," it said. "You have always been tuned in."

And God help him Jack loved it.

The thrill of it, the dark power galloping through his veins like a black stallion made of thunder and teeth. It roused something ancient in him, some worm curled around his heart. The Mouth didn't just possess him it understood him. The rage. The yearning. The rot. What could recovery offer him but light and mercy and tedious, hollow absolution?

He didn't want to be healed.

He wanted to burn.

Across Thunder Bay, radios switched on of their own accord. In the homes of the grieving, in the back rooms of hospitals, in cellars and churches and schools every speaker opened its mouth.

And screamed.

No music. No words. Just a howl. A pitch that bypassed the ears and bored straight into the soul. Windows shattered. Dogs howled. A man in a nursing home bit off his own fingers trying to make it stop.

Jack watched it all in a vision not his own.

He saw mouths erupting from transistor radios, stretching across ceilings like tumors of flesh and wire. He saw babies born with no mouths at all. He saw a woman praying in tongues, only for her jaw to fall off midhymn.

And he saw Asha.

She was marked.

Not by the Mouth but by the Seal of Light. The Aegis had chosen her, cloaked her. In a room lit by candlelight and desperation, she knelt with the others, her face blood-marked, her voice lifted in agony. They had been praying for him. For Jack.

That's when he knew.

He was not a host. He had never been. He was a conduit a pipe carved open by grief and desperation, through which the Mouth had poured its poison into the world. Claire's voice was a trap, carved from his own memories and stitched together with lies. She had never answered. She was never there.

The Mouth had lied.

Jack fell to his knees. Tears carved rivers down his cracked face. The static in his head became a scream a choir of all the souls the Mouth had devoured, howling his name with hatred and need.

But then, something shifted.

The air shimmered.

A hand extended into the studio light radiant, pure, trembling with sorrow. It wasn't loud. It wasn't dramatic. Just a presence that stilled everything for one breathless moment.

"Jack," said a voice that didn't echo. It resonated.

It was Logos.

Jack looked up, eyes full of ruin. The studio flickered between worlds. In one, he sat in a decaying broadcast room. On the other hand, he was already buried in fire and teeth.

"Jack," Logos said again. "It's not too late. You are still mine if you choose to be."

He wanted to reach. God, he wanted to reach.

But Jack laughed bitter, hollow. What was mercy to him now? He had tasted something more intoxicating than grace. The Mouth sang in him. It thrummed with promises of endless power, endless reunion, and endless voice.

Light? Love? Forgiveness?

He'd never liked the light. It had always made him feel smaller. Dirtier. Exposed.

Darkness had always fueled him.

But in the flicker of a heartbeat, he saw.

Claire.

Not as he remembered her.

But suffering.

Somewhere beyond the veil, burning, writhing, screaming in silence. Her soul was in hell. And not with the Mouth. Trapped elsewhere. Alone.

And Jack knew.

It was too late.

He'd been lied to. Used. He would never hear her voice again. Not truly. The Mouth didn't reunite it devoured. It hollowed. It wore faces like veils.

Still... he couldn't turn back.

"If she's in hell," Jack whispered, shivering, "then I go to hell."

He turned from Logos.

He took the mic in both hands and screamed into it his name, Claire's name, the names of all the damned and the Mouth howled in delight.

The studio cracked.

The words fell heavy, like the final nail in a coffin. And with that, the Mouth Beneath swept through him, flooding every inch of his being.

The transformation was slow at first, with a suffocating tightness in his chest and the skin of his face stretching unnaturally. His jaw locked, muscles grinding under the pressure. His body arched as the Mouth claimed him entirely, his form bending beneath its weight.

And then, from within the hollow of his chest, the first of the cursed words bled out. A voice, no longer his own, poured from Jack's throat deep and ancient, reverberating in tones not meant for mortal ears.

"My grief knoweth no bounds..."

It was a chant, a dirge, a promise of damnation. The words came with a rhythm that surged like a storm, the syllables dripping with cold venom. And with every word, the Mouth Beneath grew stronger, its hunger insatiable, devouring Jack's humanity with each breath.

The poem spilled from him like bile, each line more grotesque than the last, filling the studio with its dreadful weight:

"My grief knoweth no bounds
In destruction, I am found
'Tis a melody so sweet
Now in Sheol, my soul shall bask
Till the rocks of time have ticked
And the damned pour out in sheets
But beware the gleam in our eye
For we give no quarter nigh."

As the final word lingered in the air, Jack's body convulsed. His mouth stretched wide unnaturally wide as though something monstrous was clawing to break free. His eyes rolled back, and the room around him seemed to distort, bending to the will of the dark power that had overtaken him. The sounds of the broadcast, the agonized wails of the damned, bled together in a chorus of horror, filling the space.

This was the end. Not just for him, but for Thunder Bay

Flames did not erupt, but voices did spiraling into the sky, turning Thunder Bay into a cathedral of agony. All across the town, radios bled. Speakers twisted into mouths with teeth. One by one, the homes of the unprotected were swallowed.

And in the sky, Logos wept.

Not with anger.

With love.

He turned from the burning town, arms still open, still waiting.

Just in case.

But Jack was gone.

The last thing he saw before the darkness took him was a glimpse of Claire, far off, across a gulf of shadow, looking back, screaming his name in warning, not welcome.

And then the Mouth closed around him.

And the dead channel went silent.

10

The Silence of the Mouth

Thunder Bay had become a city of ghosts.

Asha had walked through it for hours, her boots scraping the icy earth, her breath twisting into cold clouds. The streets were lined with vacant houses, boarded up, storefronts empty, and cars left to rust on the curbs. It was as though the town had been hollowed out, abandoned in one silent exhale. She could feel the weight of the air, the residue of the Mouth Beneath clinging to everything. The static still lingered, clinging to her skin like an invisible coat of fear.

But Asha knew what she had to do.

The pieces were all in place now, every broken fragment of truth fitting together like a grisly puzzle. She could see it all the history of the land, the wrongs committed, the blood spilled, the ancient curses stitched into the earth like poisoned thread. The Mouth Beneath had fed on it, had become it, and now, it was a force too powerful to be contained.

The transmitter was the key.

With the last of her strength, Asha had traveled through the dead town to the radio station, Jack's sanctuary, now twisted by madness and death. Her plan was simple: destroy the transmitter, destroy the Mouth. Silence the signal. But she knew it would not be easy.

It never was.

As she stepped through the station's threshold, the air hummed with an unnatural vibration, thick, warm, and oppressive. The room was dark, lit only by the dying glow of red candles. The microphone sat in the center of a circle, pulsing like a blackened heart.

And there, standing in front of it, was Jack.

He was no longer the man she had once known. He had changed. His body, his flesh, was contorted, twisted into a grotesque mockery of what he had been. His arms stretched out at impossible angles, his face a mask of agony, his mouth wide and deformed, drooling with blackened ichor. His eyes had disappeared, leaving empty sockets that bled static.

The Mouth Beneath had taken complete control.

Asha could feel it in the air, the horrible, crushing weight of the entity inside him. It was suffocating her, clawing at her chest, as though it sought to drag her into the dark hole that now consumed Jack.

"You can't stop it," the Mouth's voice rumbled from Jack's throat. It was a sickening thing, a low, guttural sound, full of echoes and screams. "You never could."

Asha felt her resolve harden, her grip tightening on the weapon she had brought, the small, jagged shard of glass from the old records she had found at the station. The weapon was simple, but it was all she had. She stepped forward, her breath shallow, her heart pounding in her chest.

"I will stop it," she whispered. "I will stop you."

Jack's body twisted in impossible ways, the bones cracking and reforming. He was no longer human; he was a vessel for the Mouth Beneath, a puppet dancing on strings of sound and pain. His mouth stretched wide, too wide, cracking open like a cavern of teeth and shadows.

"You'll never reach it in time," the Mouth jeered. "The final tone will finish soon. The town is already mine."

Asha's fingers trembled as she moved toward the transmitter. She could hear the static swelling behind her, the sound of the Mouth gathering its power. The pulse of the radio, the signal that had claimed them all, was growing louder, pounding like a drum, like the beating of a heart.

Suddenly, Jack lunged forward, his body jerking violently. He grinned, or rather, his face twisted into something that might have been a grin. His mouth stretched unnaturally, his jaw unhinging, and he spat out a flood of blackened goo that sizzled and hissed.

Asha threw herself to the side, narrowly avoiding the burning spray. She couldn't stop now. She had to reach the transmitter.

But the Mouth Beneath was too powerful.

As she neared the equipment, Jack's body began to twist and contort in ways that should have been impossible. His limbs elongated, his chest bloated, and his face morphed into something unrecognizable. The black ichor that spilled from his mouth thickened, forming into twisted tendrils that reached for her, wrapping around her limbs, pulling her closer.

"You will never silence me," the Mouth hissed. "I will devour your soul. I will tear you apart piece by piece."

Jack's eyes returned no, the empty sockets were now filled with shadows, swirling with darkness. His mouth, once human, now yawned wide, a cavernous void that seemed to swallow the room.

Asha fought against the tendrils, trying to reach the transmitter. She knew the only way to stop this was to destroy it, to cut off the signal before the final tone could finish. But Jack was upon her now, his mouth expanding, consuming the space around him, turning into a monstrous maw. The static reached a fever pitch, and the walls of the station began to buckle.

"You can't win," the Mouth laughed, Jack's voice now twisted and alien. "You will be my feast."

Just as Jack lunged, his body becoming an impossible heap of twisted flesh and shadow, something else intervened.

The Aegis.

Asha felt a surge of light, a brilliant burst that ripped through the station like a divine force. The tendrils recoiled in agony. Jack's monstrous body froze mid-lunge as if time had been stolen from him. The Aegis's light enveloped Asha, forming a shield around her that kept the Mouth's power at bay.

But it wasn't enough.

The Mouth Beneath was too strong. Even the Aegis could not hold the darkness at bay forever.

Asha reached for the shard of glass one last time, her hands trembling with a mixture of fear and resolve. She slammed it into the transmitter's core. The world shuddered, and for a brief, fleeting moment, the static seemed to fade.

But it was too late.

With a scream of pure, primal fury, Jack's mouth expanded to unimaginable proportions, wider than any human mouth should ever have been. It split open, his flesh contorting into a grotesque parody of life. His form grew larger, a mass of writhing, blackened flesh, a mouth within a mouth.

Asha closed her eyes, bracing for what was to come.

Then, in an instant, she disappeared.

Taken by the light.

The Aegis, in their mercy, whisked her away, along with all those whose light they had protected. And the Mouth Beneath, deprived of its final prize, howled in despair.

When the light faded, Thunder Bay was empty.

Jack stood alone amidst the ruin.

The dead were scattered around him, hundreds, maybe thousands, their bodies still warm from the torment of the Mouth. But Jack remained, a twisted remnant of what he had once been. His eyes were vacant, his mouth still open, his body contorted into a demon's form.

And somewhere, deep within, the Mouth wept.

It had lost, but it would wait.

For the madness would not end.

Not until Jack's suffering had consumed him entirely.

And so, the town remained abandoned, forgotten by time, but never by the Mouth. It would always hunger.

And Jack would suffer for as long as it took.

Epilogue: The Open Mouth

"And the voice opened the earth,
And the mouths of the dead sang;
not praises, but hunger."
 The Broadcast Gospel, Verse I
Thunder Bay was dead.

Its streets were silent, but not with peace. The silence was thick pressurized, like the pause before a scream. The buildings leaned, eyes hollow, their windows smeared with ash and blood. The snow never settled. The wind never stopped. And in the heart of the ruined town, in a station long since swallowed by decay, something still moved.

Jack.

Once a man. Now... not.

He was curled beneath the old desk in the broadcast studio, ribs cracked from where the Mouth had twisted his spine in ecstasy and wrath. His voice had been flayed long ago, but still, it whimpered, low and fractured.

"Logos... I I didn't mean "
But the static answered first.

"You're not alone. We're all here.
The Mouth Beneath returned.

It did not arrive with trumpets or flames. It came as a breeze through a speaker grille, a hum inside the marrow. Jack screamed as his body seized, lifted, and slammed into the wall hard enough to crack cement. Blood burst from his mouth and eyes. He clawed at his own throat, trying to silence it but the song was inside him now.

And then the Voice came. Calm. Cold. Sad.

"Foolish mortal.

Logos offered you a hand.

A chance.

One we the Twelve would rip the heavens apart to have.

But you, the spoiled son of clay...

You refused."

Jack sobbed as the Mouth dragged his soul forward again, its presence crashing through his bones like black lightning. He remembered Logos's hand reaching for him, remembered the warmth, the gentleness. He had refused it. Not out of hate but because he could not imagine heaven without her.

"Claire..." he wept. "If she's in hell... I'll go to hell."

The Mouth laughed not loud, but broken. Pitying.

Then it split his jaw wide not metaphor, but flesh until it hung open like a curtain of meat, exposing tongue and throat. Jack gurgled and begged. The spirit lifted him again, spun him like a toy, slammed him onto the altar, where microphones twisted like vines and pierced into his chest.

"Static is the sound of something listening.

Speak.

Sing.

Bleed.

It hears you."

Jack's body jerked, bent backward until he looked like a broken crucifix. His mind teetered on madness. He thought of Claire screaming, burning. He thought of Asha her eyes just before she vanished in the light. He thought of Logos, who had offered him grace.

But he loved the Mouth.

He loved the way it thundered through him, how it gave him power the rush of being a god's throat. Logos had offered love. But love was light, and Jack had always been drawn to shadow. The Mouth offered clarity. Cruelty. Desire.

He chose it.

Even now, as his body cracked and burst, even now as he screamed

"If you're hearing this...

You're already open."

The studio glowed with sick light. The altar pulsed. In the sky above the dead town, radios still clicked on by themselves, whispering backwards prayers.

And Jack, broken and stitched by static, continued to speak.

Author's Note

My mother loves listening to the radio.

I hated it, it overstimulated me, made the walls feel like they were

breathing, and the static in my skull grew louder with every hum. Like clockwork, I would wake up to the sound of static at 3 AM in pitch blackness,

scared to death. My mind would whisper, Showtime, and begin filling in the

spaces, making things up, terrible things. I'd muster the courage to tiptoe through the dark and turn off the radio, heart hammering in my chest. But

the moment I touched the dial, my mother would wake up without fail. Why

are you touching my radio? She'd say, as if the signal itself had alerted her.

So naturally, I wrote a book about cursed radio signals at 3 AM because What else does one do when sleep is no longer a refuge?

This book was written during the quietest hours of the night, when even the

clocks seemed too afraid to tick, as though time itself was trying to escape. I

bled onto every page, dragging poems from the marrow of sadness, whispering to ghosts who, in return, whispered back with knowing eyes and trembling voices.

To those who feel unheard, unseen, or haunted, I see you.

(And I'm sorry, but so does the Mouth Beneath.)

Appendix: Lore of the Dead Channel

The Broadcast Lexicon

The Mouth Beneath
/ðə maʊθ bəˈniːθ/
A primordial, sound-based parasitic god sealed beneath Thunder Bay.
It devours not just bodies, but *belief*.
When awakened through ritual broadcasts, it feeds on pain, using grief as its gateway.

Logos
/ˈloʊˌɡoʊs/
The divine order. The opposite of chaos.
Logos offers redemption, but only through surrender and silence.
Asha walks this path.
Jack turns away.

The Aegis
/ˈiːdʒɪs/
Beings of light who shield marked souls.
They cannot destroy the Mouth but they can veil mortals from its reach
and deliver them from the edge of oblivion.

Claire's Voice
/klɛərz vɔɪs/
Not Claire.
Only an echo. A mimicry shaped by Jack's grief.
Crafted by the Mouth to ensnare him
It speaks only what he longs to hear.

The Dead Channel (Frequency 0.0)
/ðə dɛd 'tʃænəl/ – /'friːkwənsi 'zɪərəʊ/
A signal that does not exist on earthly dials.
Heard only in moments of despair, madness, or death.
Once opened, it spreads through radios, phones, and dreams.

The Furnace Mouth Mine
/'fɜrnɪs maʊθ maɪn/
Site of an old massacre.
The miners unearthed ore that *sang* in their veins.
The collapse sealed it briefly.
But buried power never stays quiet.

Final Transmission Ritual
/'faɪnəl træns'mɪʃən 'rɪtʃuəl/
Jack's broadcasts weren't just noise.
They were a sigil stretched across time
Forged through his poetry, his pain, and his grief.

The final transmission completed the circuit.
And tore the veil wide open.

WCRX

/dɛd ˈstætɪk/

(Dead Static) **noun** (forbidden)

1. A defunct, unregistered radio station believed to be a spiritual transmitter for the dead, the damned, and the forgotten.

2. Known only to appear at 103.6 FM during "thin hours" (typically between 2:47–3:33 AM), when the veil is weakest.

3. Some interpret the acronym as *We Control Restless eXiles*, *Whispers Channel Resurrection X*, or *We Can Raise the eXiled*.

4. No official records of WCRX exist. Tuning in may result in hallucinations, grief distortions, or spiritual possession.

www.ingramcontent.com/pod-product-compliance
Lightning Source LLC
Chambersburg PA
CBHW031308120726

47906CB00003B/941